Rescue Me

ANDI JAXON

This is a work of fiction. Names, characters, places, and incidents either are the product of the author's imagination or are used fictitiously. Any resemblance to actual persons, living or dead, events, or locales is entirely coincidental.

Copyright © 2020 by Andi Jaxon

All rights reserved. No part of this book may be reproduced or used in any manner without written permission of the copyright owner except for the use of quotations in a book review. For more information, address:
authorandijaxon@gmail.com

Cover design – Andi Jaxon
Paperback formatting by Just write. Creations and Services
Edited by Jenny Dillion with Prose Editing
Proofed by Jess Rousseau with Elemental Editing & Proofreading
and Emma Mack with Ultra Editing Co

www.andijaxon.com

Dedication

This book is for anyone who has ever thought they are unlovable. Your person is out there somewhere, don't give up.

One

ALISTER

Since starting here at Seattle Pacific University four years ago, the percentage of students taking Calculus has gone up twenty percent, most of which are female. For any university, it's a major increase, especially for a male-dominated subject. I wish I could say it was all because of my amazing teaching style, but in reality, it's the way my ass fills out a pair of jeans. Female students flock to my classes, and lines of fawning young women clog up the hallway during my office hours.

My shapely ass may have been what brought them in, but my teaching skills get most to pass. I take a lot of pride in my passing rates, teaching young adults to understand mathematics and its beauty gives my life meaning. When the light goes on in the head of a struggling student, the pieces click together, and I'm high on life.

Working at a Christian university isn't the finest idea for a gay man, but since I'm unattached, and plan to keep it that way for a while, it's not a big deal. Sure, I've dated, I'm no blushing virgin, but it's always been casual friends who engage in sex. Someday I want the emotional connection my parents have. They are the best example that I can think of, of a happy and healthy marriage, living with them instilled the idea into my twin brother and me of wanting a relationship like theirs.

I live close to campus, walk everywhere I'm able to, and hit the gym a few times a week to make sure I take care of myself. I'm not afraid to say I think I'm attractive and well dressed, I'm not overly cocky, I have the self-confidence my mother ingrained in me. At this point in my career, I don't care what brings the students in, as long as they learn something.

I walk the fifteen minutes to campus to prepare for the first day of the semester, because I'm excited like I always am. Colorful foliage and lush trees always brings a smile to my face. It's beautiful here. Classic brick buildings with a modern flair brings this small university its own personality. Students crowd brick pathways, both new and returning, as they meet friends and find where their classes are. The first week is always invigorating, especially during the fall semester, it's a new year, and everyone is full of hope. Will my classes be kids fresh out of high school, eager to learn, or a group of students who have been putting off math for years and no longer remember any algebra? Both come with their advantages and disadvantages. Younger kids tend to screw around on their phones and want to argue failing grades, while the older students are desperate to pass.

In early September, the air is crisp here in Western Washington, and the wind coming off Lake Union is making it colder. The leaves are starting to turn yellow, orange, and red, the sunset is getting earlier, and the rain is returning. It's almost time for scarves, beanies, and hot soup.

"Morning ladies," I tell the staff in the copying office, smiling at my favorite person on campus.

"Alister, my future ex-husband, I've got your copies right here, love," Darla, the supervisor, says when she sees me. She's a great lady, always ready to laugh but never takes crap from anyone. She's on the short side, graying, and pushing sixty. Her grandkids are her life, and though she's been married half a dozen times, she doesn't seem to dwell on her divorces. She's also a shameless flirt, gives the best hugs, and is the best person to have in your corner during a fight.

"Good morning, Mr. Bennet," a young student worker says, a blush on her cheeks, her voice barely more than a whisper. I give the girl a smile and a wink when I see Darla heading my way with a stack of papers.

She rolls her eyes and shakes her head behind the girl. "If you're winking at anyone, it had better be me. Don't tell me you're straying away from me already?" she teases, with a laugh sparkling in her eyes.

"I would be the luckiest man in the world to come home to you every night." She hands me the papers and I kiss her cheek. "Until next time." With a smile on my face and a bounce in my step, I head to my office to get situated. As I walk down the hallway, my shoes clacking against the polished hardwood floors, I notice someone sits outside my office door. Someone in dark jeans, ripped at the knees, well-worn converse, and a black hoodie pulled over their head, hiding their face. Upon hearing my approach, they turn and pierce me with deep pools of onyx. My breathing halts as if the oxygen was sucked from the room.

He's out of place here among the halls of this university. He's darker than most of the students here, not his skin color or clothes, but him. His eyes tell a story of pain, a story I want to know so that I can soothe his broken and bleeding soul. I've never seen anyone with eyes like this and I can't look away. I don't know what this young man has been through, but I suddenly want to be his safe harbor during the storm.

He rushes to stand once he sees me approaching, a few inches shorter than my 6'2" height, on the scrawny side, and with a warm complexion. He's nervous but trying not to show it, chewing on his thick lower lip is a dead giveaway though. I need to tell him it's okay, I don't bite, but I doubt it would go over well. *Why do I want to reach out and hug him?* I'm not a big touchy-feely kind of guy, but I crave to touch him. I've never been attracted to a student before, but this one has a magnetism I can't ignore. I clear my throat and offer him a smile he doesn't return.

Two

BEN

THE CLICK-CLACK OF shoes on the wood floor alerts me to someone approaching, I glance up and see *him*. Alister Bennet. Calculus teacher and the man starring in my dreams. He's temptation in human form and everything I can't have. His black hair is short on the sides with a good few inches on top to twist my fingers in, he has a scruffy black beard, and his bright eyes make his olive skin look impossibly soft. My fingers itch to run through his hair and my lips tingle at the thought of his facial hair prickling my skin as he kisses me.

His movements are confident, almost cocky, completely sure of with who he is. As if life is a dance he already knows the steps to. I can't stop the images flashing in my head of him fucking a girl beneath him, mindless with pleasure at his expertise, the way his hips and ass flex as he thrusts, giving as much pleasure as he's taking. I'm not attracted to girls, but the image makes my dick twitch. Everything about him makes my dick twitch, if I'm being honest. I shouldn't be attracted to him, it's wrong.

His broad chest is always on display in his well-fitted, button-up shirts, the top two or three buttons open at the throat to show the muscles and soft, dark hair. Every part of him is ripped with muscle: forearms, shoulders, thighs, ass. His jeans look like they were made just for him, how I wish I could slide my hands into his back pockets to grip his ass and press myself against him. His eyes meet mine when they look up at him, and I know he's seeing the torn, ragged edges of my soul. My normal wall, the mask I show the world to keep it out, is defenseless against him. His mere presence strips me bare.

Scrambling to my feet, I stand as he approaches his office, standing off to one side, making myself seem as small as possible in an attempt to fade into the background. It's the first day of classes, and I'm already panicking. Calculus is just not my thing. If I can't pass this class, I won't graduate. If I don't graduate, I have no money for classes next term. My scholarship runs out this term, I have to finish.

Leather satchel over his shoulder, a stack of papers in one hand and keys in the other, he clears his throat and smiles at me as he approaches the door. The warm smile wraps around my heart, melting the ice in my chest I use for protection.

"I wasn't expecting any students this early. If you could give me a second to get settled, I would be happy to talk to you." Perfectly straight white teeth show between his lips when he speaks to me.

"No problem, sorry to bother you," I mumble, not even sure he heard me.

Setting his papers on the desk and his bag to the side, he turns on his computer and has a seat. His distraction gives me time to look around the small space from the doorway. He didn't invite me in, and I know better than to enter a space I'm not invited in to, he doesn't want my perversion to taint the sanctity of his office.

A corkboard with pictures I can't make out is behind his desk, along with a bookshelf full of math books. The window next to his desk gives him a magnificent view of campus, with brick buildings, green grass, colorful trees, and the Cascade Mountains on a cloudless day. Everything is tidy and in order. The space is tiny but comfortable and smells spicy like cinnamon, nutmeg, and a hint of something rugged.

Seeing me standing in the doorway, he looks surprised to see me in the hallway. "Would you like to come in?"

Stepping over the boundary into his office feels like a big deal, looking at the floor, I'm not sure I can force my feet to move. My dirty, almost worn through the sole Converse, might leave marks on his carpet.

In a flash, I'm back in Dan's house, desperately pleading not to get beaten again. It was raining, and my shoes were muddy from the walk from the bus stop, something I noticed once I had walked onto the carpet. At ten years old, I was begging for mercy from a man incapable of showing any.

A clearing of his throat shakes the memory free, but the fear remains. Sneaking a glance at him, he's still watching me closely. I'm an idiot. I shouldn't have come here to talk to him, I knew it was a mistake. "Nah, I'm good right here." Leaning against the doorjamb, so I don't have to enter. I can't look at him yet, since my face is hot from the embarrassment of not being able to come into a room. I'm such a freak.

"Okay, what brings you to my office on the first day, two hours before I teach my first class?" His voice has my eyes lifting to his. He's trying to keep the mood lighter, making a joke and lifting his lips in a sexy smirk. I can't breathe, much less think, when that smirk is directed at me.

"I'm going to fail," blurts out of my mouth before my brain has a chance to stop it. He gets a little crease between his eyebrows, his smile drops, and his head tilts to the side. Studying me once again, his lips pursed.

"What's your name?"

"Ben Wallace," I answer automatically.

"How old are you, Ben?"

"Twenty-three." *What does my age have to do with anything?*

A smile returns to his plump lips, and I find myself sucking on my own, imagining what he tastes like.

"You must be about ready to graduate. Is that what you're afraid of? Not graduating on time?"

I'm still standing awkwardly in his office doorway, the guest chair sitting empty in front of me. I've seen him on campus numerous times and have been daydreaming about him ever since. I can't believe I'm standing here, talking to him, so close I can almost touch him. God, do I want to touch him. *Shit, what did he say?*

"Ben? Why don't you sit down?" Shaking my head to clear it, I take the few steps in and sit on the edge of the seat, too busy thinking about his lips on mine to realize what I've done.

"Could you tutor me? After classes, I could come here, to your office?"

Could I be any more awkward? What the hell is wrong with me?

"I'm happy to help clear things up during office hours, and there are tutors available, math labs you can go to if you feel you need extra help." The crease has returned between his eyebrows, I need to get out of here.

"Never mind, I'll see you around, Teach." Grabbing my bag outside the door, I keep moving down the hallway and out of the building until I can't hear him calling my name anymore. I love the way he says my name, how his lips look when he says it. I need to stay away from him, or I will end up throwing myself at him and heartbroken when he turns me down. I'm an idiot for lusting after a teacher, especially a straight one.

Three

ALISTER

I WANT TO HELP him, Ben. I could sense his anxiety over not passing my class. He tried to play it off like it wasn't a big deal, but the anxiety was there, plain as day. I wanted to reassure him, cover his hand with mine, tell him everything would be okay. He's most likely on a scholarship, and if he fails a class, he loses it.

Leaning over my chair to stretch my back, I force myself to focus on my upcoming class. Looking over the roster, half of the names appear female, and I'm betting half of those won't stick around.

Turning on the Keurig, I make myself a cup of dark roast coffee. The scent is waking me up as much as the caffeine when it hits my system. Coffee is a way of life here, and there are Starbucks and espresso stands on most street corners. Over the years I've grown to enjoy the bitter brew, I can't start a day without a cup, and I end up drinking it all day long.

Noticing the time, I grab my cup and syllabi, and head to my first class of the semester. How much time did I spend thinking about my visitor? What is it about him that's so intriguing? We barely spoke to each other and it wasn't much of a conversation. I know nothing more than his name and age, but I want to have a real conversation with him. I've dated, I'm not a recluse, but I've never reacted to someone like this. It's terrifying and exciting, and completely inappropriate. I need to stay away from him. Clearing my thoughts of Ben, I focus on my upcoming class.

Excitement hums through me. I'm not afraid to be excited about math. I'm a full fledge math nerd and proud of it. Already, there are students around the hall waiting for me to open the door. This class looks like mostly first-year students, which is good. It's less time I have to spend going over material they should already know.

Everyone starts filing in once the door is open and someone turns the lights on. My early morning visitor, Ben, keeps his head down as he finds a seat in the middle of the room. I find I'm a little disappointed when he doesn't look at me, since I want those pitch-black eyes on me again. I don't understand why I'm disappointed. I've never been one to need attention. He's a student, any feelings I have for him are completely inappropriate. My body reacts to his nearness anyway, and I struggle to keep my blood from pooling below my waist. These pants are snug and there's no way to hide a damn hard-on. With things like 'dick prints' popping up on social media, I need to get my mind on track for class.

Class begins and I introduce myself, before passing out the necessary paperwork. Taking attendance, I pause a moment when I come to his name, Ben Wallace. Like so many others, he's just trying to survive. Just get through this class and be one step closer to graduation.

"Benjamin Wallace?" His name rolls off my tongue like a lover. Finally, his head lifts, the ebony pools sucking me in from across the room.

"Ben."

I nod my head at the correction and force my eyes from his. I have never wanted to cross the line between teacher and student before, but something about him makes me want to throw caution to the wind and say, "fuck it." It's going to be an exceptionally long term keeping my hands to myself. I hope he's able to find a tutor, so I'm not cramped in my very small office with him very often. I foresee a lot of time spent with my right hand over the next few weeks, cumming to the image of that boy on his knees looking up at me, on his back with his head thrown back in ecstasy, on his hands and knees offering up his ass.

Giving myself a shake, I continue with attendance and get started.

"I'm glad you're all here, welcome to Calculus I." I force a smile and hope it looks comforting instead of predatory, which is how I'm feeling at the moment. The female population in the class swoons, so it must be alright. I'm typically an easy-going guy, not much gets me riled up. I guess I've found my kryptonite, Ben Wallace. He's a shot of adrenaline straight to my heart. I don't wish to stand here and have a polite conversation. I want to stalk my prey and fuck him until we can't stand any longer.

This is not like me at all. I'm not a dominant guy and I'm not an alpha. I'm no spineless chump, but I don't ever feel the need to go after people. I guess a good workout after-school is the plan for today. I need to work off whatever this is and get back to an even keel.

Four

BEN

All through class he looks at me, his eyes finding mine. My pulse races, raising my body temperature to something above freezing. It scares the shit out of me, but damn if it isn't an ego boost. I may spontaneously combust right here in my seat just from the look in his eyes when he says my name. He's got such a sexy voice too, a smooth tenor, like warm molasses. It's comforting and demanding all at once.

In my fantasy I can be excited at the prospect of being with him, and I can be confident and eager to please him. In reality, terror outweighs everything else. The amount of need my body already has for him, a man I don't know, scares the shit out of me. I've thought of it so many times over the last few months, but now that I've talked to him, the fantasy is so much more real. The image of my foster father, Dan, is enough to send ice through my veins, bringing me back to reality.

I tried to be straight, all through high school I tried. If it wasn't for my best friend Kristen continuing to play the part of my girlfriend after I told her I was gay, I don't think I would have made it through high school. She was a godsend, and I will never be able to repay her for everything she did for me. She was especially good at making Dan believe it was real. He even "caught" us making out a few times, it was awkward for us, but it was necessary. I'm not entirely sure he wouldn't have killed me if I had told him I was gay.

When I tell Kristen I was in *his* office this morning, she's going to want details. Every possible detail. Luckily for her, I won't forget anything, I can't. I want to know everything about him, even though I know it's a bad idea. Even if he were gay, which I guarantee he isn't, he would never want a guy like me. He's confident, refined, and mature. I'm on the verge of being homeless with no family and am basically a walking insecurity. He could do so much better than me.

Five

ALISTER

Class is dismissed, and everyone collects their things and files out. Everyone but Ben Wallace. He hasn't made a move to talk to me, so I go about cleaning off the whiteboard and organizing my things.

It was a struggle to keep my eyes off him while I went over the syllabus, since my eyes were drawn to him. I've never been attracted to anyone like this, ever. I'm starting to frustrate myself. I've had relationships in the past, but they were more friends with sex, nothing close to this overwhelming need to touch, to taste, to own. I want him in the most basic sense of the word, on a molecular level, but I also want to know him. I need to know what makes him tick, who his best friends are, what his parents were like growing up. I need to know everything about him.

I'm so caught up in my head and forcing myself to keep my eyes off him, I don't notice when he's standing in front of me. Clearing his throat, I startle when I look up and see him on the other side of the desk. He doesn't say anything, just stands there staring up at me, eyes blazing. My skin heats and my heart pounds the longer he stands there saying nothing. Since when am I unsure of myself? I'm confident of myself and my abilities, I know how to talk to students, and yet my words are failing me now.

The flush of his cheeks, and his increased breathing shows me he's just as affected as I am. His lips part and his tongue peeks out as he wets them. My eyes zero in on a flash of pink, wet flesh. I crave to feel it everywhere. I want to know what it tastes like, what it feels like on my skin.

Before I know it, he turns and walks out of the room, breaking the spell I'm under. What the hell is wrong with me? He's my student, and that's a line I refuse to cross. Shaking my head to clear the lust filled fog, I grab my briefcase and head to my office to prepare for my next class.

The entire walk back across campus, I chastise myself. This is ridiculous, he's twenty-three, I'm thirty-six. He's getting ready to graduate and go out into the world, to find out who he really is, and what he wants to do with his life. I'm settled into my life. He's not my responsibility, he's my student, and I will help him anyway I can in that respect, but nothing more.

When I get to my office, there's a message on my voicemail, probably from my mother. I dial up my inbox anyway, just to make sure it's not an important call that needs my attention.

"Good morning, Alister." My mother's soft voice sings through the line. "I hope your first day of school is a good one. Don't forget about dinner on Thursday evening. See you soon. I love you."

The message makes me smile. My mother is the sweetest woman in the entire world. She has always supported me and was the first person I came out to when I came to terms with being gay. Her response was, "Oh, well okay then. Dinner is at five, don't think this gets you out of eating your vegetables." Everything went on as normal because she treated it like it wasn't a big deal, which it wasn't.

Everything about her is soft and feminine, from her bone structure, to her attire and personality. I started my teaching career as a substitute, then worked as a high school math teacher for a few years. It wasn't until I had been working with teenagers for about six months, that I realized just how lucky I was to have her growing up. No matter what I did she would always be in my corner, which is something most of today's youth don't have. I have a feeling Ben Wallace is one of those unlucky ones.

A knock on the door startles me. "Come in."

A blushing young co-ed opens the door and stands there, just staring at me. I wish I could say this was a weird occurrence, but I've gotten used to it. I'm sure there's a line of girls halfway down the hallway already, and it's not even noon.

"Good morning, Miss…" I raise an eyebrow waiting for her to tell me her name, but she still doesn't say anything.

"Miss!" I say a little lower, hoping to shock her out of whatever trance she's in. "How can I help you?"

"I'm afraid I won't be able to pass your class. Do you tutor after hours?" Her face turns bright red, and she sucks her bottom lip into her mouth.

A sigh slips past my lips, these girls are getting bolder and bolder every year. Sometimes I wish I were an eighty-year-old, bald, chubby guy. I guarantee they don't deal with these types of propositions.

"I'm sorry, but no, I don't. If you're that concerned about passing my class, perhaps you should take an easier one."

Shame and embarrassment have her closing in on herself, and without another word, she leaves the office and disappears. I was harsher than I should have been, she didn't deserve to be talked down to. I need to get my head straight, shake off the morning and focus.

Six

BEN

I'M AN IDIOT. A goddamn idiot. I stood there and stared at him like he was an exhibit at the zoo. That's it, I can't talk directly to him. If I have a question, I'll email him so I don't have to look at him or hear him say my name.

Riding my bike back to my shit hole apartment, my phone rings and I know immediately who it is, Kristen. Pulling the phone to my ear, I smile when I see her name and picture on the screen.

"Hey, Kris, what's up?"

"Uck. You know I hate when you call me that, right?" I can picture her rolling her eyes at me.

"Yup, that's why I do it. Well, and because I've been doing it for years and it's a habit now."

"Soooo," she says, dragging out the word, "how was class?"

"You're as subtle as Niagara Falls, you know that?"

"Come on! Tell me all about the infamous Alister Bennet!" she whines, and I can picture her stomping her foot. "Pictures of him can't possibly do him justice."

"He's hot," I deadpan.

"I swear to God, Ben, I'm going to stab you while you sleep." She sounds pretty serious, and I'm forced to laugh at her. "Did you talk to him? What does he smell like? Does he have an amazing voice?"

"I'm not home yet, so you'll just have to wait." Looking around, I see thugs, homeless, and drug addicts. I'm sure I'd be a crime victim if they heard me talking about how attractive my *male* teacher is.

She sighs heavily into the phone. "I guess I can wait. How was his class? Is he only assigning homework and having tests, or will there be projects?"

"I didn't hear a word he said besides my name, I don't stand a chance of passing…"

"Well, that will definitely make tests more interesting, look at your syllabus, it'll tell you what types of things are expected from you."

It's my turn to sigh this time. "I have to pass this class. I don't have the option of failure. I should have taken the class taught by the little old lady. I guarantee I wouldn't be struggling like this in her class."

"You would be falling asleep, and you know it, plus her classes didn't fit your schedule with the other classes you have to take. You'll pass. If we have to Skype every night so I can teach you the material, we will. You know I'll help you any way I can." She's so sure, it makes me a little more confident.

"I don't have internet this semester, and my data plan had to be cut back, so I can't skype. I sold my laptop over the summer to help pay rent, the only way to work on projects is in the library."

"Jesus, Ben. Why didn't you tell me? I would have helped you, you know? I'm not going to let you be homeless and the last thing we want is for Dan to find you again." I know she would have helped me without a second thought, but I can't let anyone else have something to hold over my head. Dammit, I want to stand on my own two feet and do this myself. If it means not eating every day, or having to sell stuff to make ends meet, then that is what I will do.

"I got it handled. It wasn't a big deal."

Getting to my apartment, I carry my bike up the stairs, then dig my keys out of my pocket and let myself in, locking the door behind me. I don't live in a very safe part of town, so locked doors are just a way of life. Though in the building I live in, no one has anything worth stealing, but it doesn't stop dumb ass teenagers or druggies from trying.

"I heard your deadbolt, so spill the beans on Captain Calculus!" Kristen shrieks into my ear.

Dropping down onto my bed, I close my eyes and picture him striding down the hallway, sitting behind his desk, and standing at the front of the classroom. I start to harden. I want him. It's as simple and as complicated as that. I can't have him, he's my teacher and far above me. I'm also pretty sure he's straight. I may not have personal experience, but it doesn't mean I don't know what I want, and what I want is him.

"Hello! Earth to Ben!" I pull my phone away from my ear at her shout.

I sigh as I remember where I am. "He's amazing. He's so much taller in person, and when his attention is directed at you, all you see is him. His skin is the color of a good latte, and he smells like cinnamon and nutmeg. He's intoxicating." The last sentence is a whisper.

I'm met with silence, and for the first time in her life, Kristen is speechless. The thought makes me laugh, and once I start laughing, I can't stop. The entire situation is so ridiculous. Here I am, alone in my shit-tastic apartment, telling my best friend turned ex-girlfriend about my male math teacher who I want to have sex with. Nope, this is not at all weird.

"Tell me everything. Don't leave out any details!" she demands.

"I met him at his office, hours before class, freaking out about passing the class. I made a complete ass of myself. He probably thinks I'm a freak, a total weirdo."

"I highly doubt that. Unless you confessed your undying love to him and proposed to him on the spot." She's so matter-of-fact. "You didn't, right?"

"Of course not." Hesitating, I don't want to tell her what happened when I froze because my past choked me, but she'll know if I leave it out. "I panicked," I say, frustrated at myself.

"What happened? What tripped you up?" She knows everything about me, every sordid detail, every horror story which makes up my past.

"He had carpet in his office."

She remembers the beating I took after tracking dirt onto the carpet in Dan's house, black and blue colored my back and ribs, it's not something a ten-year-old forgets. I could barely breathe with the cracked ribs, and I missed a week of school because I had to wait for the swelling on my face to go down enough to be able to see.

"He's not Dan. Alister Bennet is a good man. From everything I found when I was writing my article about him, everyone I talked to, everything said so. You know my stalker skills are second only to the FBI."

"I know, I know. It came out of nowhere, took me by surprise. I ended up leaning against the doorjamb, like a tool. I called him "teach," Kristen. What the hell is wrong with me?"

"There is nothing wrong with you! You got flustered. It happens to everyone."

"You would think I would be used to life not being fair, but this seems so much worse than normal. Even if he was gay, which he's not, there is nothing about me that would entice a man like him. He's confident, sophisticated, and smart. What do I have to offer him? I'm nothing. I don't know why I'm even still here." I'm completely defeated by life. I am nothing, have nothing, and will never be anything.

"Are you done with your pity party?" Irritation laces her voice, even over the phone I can feel it. "You are so much more than nothing. One day, you're going to see just how important you are, and I will be there to kick you in the ass."

"Sorry, it's been a long day. I need to get this studying done. Call you later?" If I were straight, I would have taken her off the market a long fucking time ago. It's not like I didn't try either. We dated for about a minute and a half our freshmen year but kept up the charade all four years to try and fool Dan into thinking I was straight. It made life a lot easier.

"I got a hot date tonight. I'll call you after," she giggles, and I know I'm forgiven.

"Send me pictures!"

Seven

ALISTER

THURSDAY NIGHT DINNERS ARE a tradition in the Bennet house. Since the time we were busy with after-school activities, my mom has made it mandatory for us to get together one night a week and eat dinner as a family. The day of the week has changed over the years as schedules changed, but since Alexander and I left for college, it's been Thursday night.

I reach for the door handle, but it opens before I can grab it. The shit eating grin of my twin brother appears in the doorway.

"Beat ya," he says, his smug smirk firmly in place, arms crossed over his chest.

"There was a crash on 522," I smartly tell him. My twin brother and I have had this strange competition since we were old enough to drive, the first one home wins bragging rights, I don't even remember why or how it started anymore.

Shouldering my way past him, I hear my mother in the kitchen singing and my father yelling at the football game on TV and I smile at the familiarity, some things never change.

"Alister! I'm so glad you're here!" My mother lifts her cheek for me to kiss while she stirs the marinara on the stove. She makes everyone feel important, it doesn't matter if she saw you yesterday, or a year ago, her reaction is always the same. Everyone is always welcome at her table, doesn't matter if you're a janitor or a CEO, she'll feed you all the same. I know exactly how blessed I am to have her.

"Oh, Alister." She holds the flowers with both hands and buries her face in the colorful blooms. "They're beautiful, thank you, dear."

Putting the beer I brought into the fridge, I step up to the stove and stir the sauce as my mother goes about putting the flowers in water. There have always been fresh flowers in our house.

"How are classes going, Ali?" mother asks over her shoulder.

"So far, so good."

"Meet anyone that catches your interest?" Instantly, Ben and his brooding, dark looks come to mind. His magnetic energy I can't seem to break away from.

"Hmmm…" She hums knowingly.

"It's nothing Mom, just an interesting student is all." I try and fail to make it out to be no big deal. Unfortunately, she sees right through me. She always could.

"What's his name?" She's turned to look at me, hands folded in front of her. I know this look well, and it means I'm not going anywhere until I tell her everything she wants to know. Luckily, I know how to get around her therapist tricks.

"Oh no! Sorry, Mom, I think the sauce is sticking!" I fake panic.

Huffing at me, she swats me away from the stove to watch football with Alex and Dad. Alister – 1, Mom – 0.

Somewhere between standing and sitting, my adoring brother pipes up, "Got yourself a boyfriend?"

"No, I don't. One of my students this term is interesting, nothing more." The smirk on his face says he's not done ribbing me yet, and I guarantee he's going to get Mom going again too. Dad raises an eyebrow but doesn't comment.

"Any hot chicks *desperate* to pass your class yet?" Alexander, the man-whore everyone.

"Stay away from my students. Having sex with you will guarantee them a failing grade." I smirk back at him. Dad coughs to cover his chuckle. I don't know why he does it, we have known for most of our lives he's laughing at us.

"Perhaps they need the comforting after you undoubtingly crushed their dreams of passing this much-needed class?" He wags his eyebrows at me, laughing.

"Been that long since you got laid that you have to go sniffing around after eighteen-year-old children?" I quip, folding my arms over my chest.

"Hey, eighteen means they're legal, brother," he retorts, pointing a finger at me. Dad's coughing fit seems to have gotten worse, his face is now bright red, and he's shaking from the force of his cough, but he's smiling.

"Hey, I'm just trying to spend quality time with our old man, watching the Seahawks kill… uh, whoever this is," I say, turning away from Alex and focusing on the TV.

"Alister, don't think I've forgotten what we were talking about!" Mother's voice singsongs from behind me.

"He said he's got a boyfriend, Mom!" Alex hollers over his shoulder, laughing into his hand. I swear, the second we both get into this house, we are no longer adults but fifteen years old again.

"Just wait until you bring a girl home, you're going to pray for death," I whisper so only he and Dad can hear me.

Mom comes out of the kitchen with hands on her hips. "Why didn't you bring him to dinner?" Not bring my imaginary boyfriend to dinner has offended her, great.

"I do *not* have a boyfriend. Alex is being an ass."

"Language!" she scolds. "Dinner is ready, turn off the TV please, David."

Dinner consists of freshly made salad, garlic bread, and spaghetti with my mother's famous sauce. Mother, of course, chooses the moment my mouth is full to start asking me questions.

"Alister, what is his name?"

I glare at Alex while I chew, his smirk clear. "Mother, I don't have a boyfriend. One of my students is an interesting person, but they are a student and therefore not a dating possibility, even if I was interested in dating them, which I'm not."

Looking up at her, she is still expecting a name.

"Ben. He's twenty-three, taking his last classes before graduation, and is scared of losing his scholarship." Alex is snickering, so I shoot him another glare.

"Well, you should bring him to dinner. I would like to meet him."

"That's completely inappropriate. I can't invite a student to my parents' house."

It's her turn to sigh, and lifting her glass to her lips, she eyes me while she sips her wine. She's plotting a way to make this happen. This is going to be bad for me.

Eight

BEN

AFTER A WARMISH SHOWER, I'M huddled in bed with a flashlight and homework. It's freezing in here, but I can't afford to turn on the heat. Unfortunately, I'm also out of ramen, and my blanket is at least a decade old.

Having wet hair is not helping me at all, and my hands are shaking, so my writing is almost illegible. Fuck it, I'm not doing any more homework right now.

Grabbing my extra hoodie, I pull it on over the one I'm already wearing and curl up under my threadbare blanket. Someday I'll have a safe place to live, be able to eat real food, and stay warm. Maybe I'll even get to take hot showers.

Closing my eyes, I try to ignore my hungry stomach and force myself to sleep. Grumbling and starting to cramp, hunger pains aren't anything I'm unfamiliar with.

Unfortunately, closing my eyes has me picturing Alister. I groan as blood surges to my dick.

Rolling onto my back, I don't stop myself from imagining him here with me, keeping me warm with his body against mine. Reaching into my sweats, I wrap my fist around my dick and stroke it. Picturing his hands in my hair, lips claiming mine, his hard cock rubbing against mine while my thighs cradle his hips.

My hips jerk, cinnamon and nutmeg surrounding my memory of him as my vision changes. Now, he's inside me, stretching my hole. Spurts of hot cum shoot onto my stomach when he's as deep as he can be, thighs against my ass, then flexes to make me take just a centimeter more while his bright eyes are darkened with arousal.

Out of breath, I throw my arm over my eyes. What kind of masochist falls for someone unavailable to him? I'm going to hell for lusting after a man. It's unnatural, wrong. I hate that I can't just be right, be attracted to girls like I should be.

At least I'm not cold anymore.

Grabbing a shirt off the floor, I wipe up the mess and fall into a deep sleep for the first time in weeks.

Nine

ALISTER

15 Days Later

It's Friday evening, and I'm heading home after a long week of classes, I can already taste the cold, dark beer sitting in my fridge. I'll turn on an episode of Game of Thrones, have dinner, and enjoy the Irish Death waiting for me while pretending Ben's eyes on me every class isn't eating away at me. He always sits in the back row of the class, as far away from me as he can get, never asks any questions. He turns in his assignments without a glance at me, accepts any returned work without a word, and is always careful not to touch my hand. He's not doing well, he needs a tutor, but I doubt he'll use one. If he doesn't do something soon, he's not going to pass the class.

Lost in thought about a student I care too much for, I almost miss the commotion in front of the library.

"Please! I just need another hour! I have to finish!" *I know that voice, it haunts my dreams...* the desperation and fear go straight to my gut.

"I'm sorry, but we're closed, you have to go home," the librarian says with her arms crossed over her chest, two security guards in front of her. Since I saw someone get up off the ground, it's clear they physically removed him from the building.

From across the lawn, I can tell he's tense. His hands are running through this hair over and over as he tries to calm his nerves. Something isn't right here, and I can't stand by and let them manhandle him. With my bag thrown over my shoulder, I break into a jog toward them. The closer I get, the more I notice about the situation. He's not just tense, he looks on the edge of a breakdown. He's breathing too fast, pacing like a caged animal. *What is going on with him?*

"Ben," I holler as I get closer to him. He spins around and pierces me with his stare. "What's going on?"

Panic and frustration fill his eyes, and his hands go back to his hair and pull on the shaggy locks. "I need to finish my outline for my paper, but she kicked me out! Literally, they threw me out! The outline is due tonight, and this is the only place I can work on it." He sounds on the verge of tears and it breaks my heart.

"You should have thought of that before the night it was due!" Mrs. Carter's shrill voice shouts over her shoulder as she makes her way back inside.

Without thinking it through, I put my hands on his shoulders, so he's facing me. "Come on. I've got a place you can work on your paper."

His eyes snap to mine, searching for something, then wrapping his arms around my chest, he hugs me, saying "thank you" into my chest. For a moment I'm too shocked to move, but slowly, my hands sweep along his back, and I hug him to me. His hair smells like rain, his sweater like musk and laundry soap, it's a heady mixture I'm trying as hard as I can to ignore. His body is flush against mine and I can tell how thin he is, even through his sweater I can feel the indents between his ribs. When a shudder rushes through him, it sets off goosebumps across my skin.

Laughter nearby shakes me from the cocoon I'm enveloped in where only the two of us exist. We're on campus. I can't be seen embracing a student like this, especially a male student. This entire situation, me offering him a place to study, has to stay between the two of us, or I'll be fired so fast my head will spin.

Stepping away from him, I clear my throat and awkwardly pat his shoulder. "Ahem, grab your backpack and come with me. You can study where I'm going."

Fixing his hood back over his hair, he grabs his bag off the steps, no doubt where it landed after being thrown, and shoves his hands into the hoodie pocket. It seems strange he's not asking me where I'm leading him, I could be a serial killer for all he knows. Perhaps he's too grateful for the opportunity to finish his homework, and he's afraid to ask questions, for fear of me changing my mind or of seeming ungrateful.

I slow my pace until he's walking next to me, looking around to make sure no one will overhear me, I whisper, "I live right off campus, within walking distance."

Surprise brings his brows together, but he stares intently at me for a moment before he nods. He tenses again, the air between us awkward. I'm sure he's thinking I'm some kind of pervert only helping him to get sexual favors from him, or leading him into a trap to have him beat up, but we can't have this conversation here. It will just have to wait until I can guarantee no one overhears us.

Ten

BEN

HIS HOUSE? IS HE *taking me to his house?*

I don't know what to think about this, about him allowing me into his home, even the fact he offered is mind-blowing. Is there a catch? This feels like a trap. The only person that has ever helped me is Kristen. What is he going to want from me in exchange for his help? The thought of him wanting sexual favors for payment isn't as distasteful as it should be. But he isn't gay, so I can't picture what he could possibly want from me. Except he hugged me, in front of the library, he hugged me like I mattered, and for just a second, I let myself believe I did.

Walking beside him is awkward, because he's so much bigger than me, it looks like I'm walking with my dad. If this damn paper wasn't so important, I would blow it off or would have sent what I had when the damn librarian kicked me out, but it's worth half of my grade.

We enter a nice building, obviously well maintained and expensive. I already feel out of place, and we're just in the hallway. My stomach is in knots, partly from not knowing what will happen when we reach his apartment and partly from hunger. I ate half of a bagel this morning, the last of yesterday's meal. Hopefully, my scholarship will come through soon so I can get some groceries.

Opening the door, Alister walks in, turning on lights as he goes. I want to follow him, but he has light colored carpet, and my boots are dirty. Again, I'm afraid I'll leave footprints on his perfect floor. I would take them off, but I'm sure my socks stink, not to mention the holes in them. These are the only dry socks I had, so even though I wore them yesterday, I had to wear them again today or get blisters from not wearing any.

"Ben?"

Looking up, Alister is standing at the end of entryway hall his brows pulled together. "Are you going to come in?"

"My boots are dirty." Before thinking of a good answer, words tumble from my mouth. *Could I be any more awkward?*

"It's alright. I'm going to get the carpets cleaned next week anyway. Come on in, have a seat."

Waving me in, I decided to take his word for it and enter the apartment, closing the door softly behind me. I hear the heater turn on and am hit with a pang of jealousy, not only do I have to keep the heat turned off ninety percent of the time, I only have one light on at a time too.

Everything in this place says comfort and class, money. Overstuffed dark leather couch and recliners, solid wood tables, and a huge TV mounted to the wall. Soft blue blankets are folded over the back of the couch and each recliner and a large family picture is centered on the wall behind it. Alister, his parents, his brother, they look so much alike, they could be the same person, twins. They look happy, smiling, with laughter in their eyes, love obvious in the way they stand together with arms around each other. I always wanted that, a family to love me. Instead, I was wrapped in a dirty blanket and left in a dumpster behind a restaurant. I'm not sure if I'm grateful or angry that a bus-boy heard me crying and found me.

Turning toward the sounds in the kitchen, Alister comes out with two bottles of water and hands one to me.

"Go ahead and get comfortable, there's a plug next to the couch for your laptop, and when you're ready. I'll get you signed into the Wi-Fi."

Shame colors my cheeks, looking at my boots, I inform him of my situation. "I don't have a laptop."

"Oh. How do you normally do your homework?" I don't hear judgment, just intrigue. Risking a glance at him, I notice he's watching me curiously.

"In the library, it's my only option."

"Hmm, okay. I'll grab mine for you."

He disappears down the hallway into what I assume is either his bedroom or an office, rummages around for a minute, then comes back. "Would you prefer to work at a table where you can spread out, or here in the living room where it's more comfortable?"

"It doesn't matter, beggars can't be choosers. Thanks." Sitting down in the closest recliner, I sink into the buttery soft leather and cushioning surrounding me. A grateful groan escapes my lips without my meaning to. Hearing a chuckle, I look up and see that Alister is standing in front of me with that damn smirk on his lips again, holding the laptop out to me. Clearing my throat, I sit up and set my bag on the floor and sign into my school account to find my essay. I can't help but stare at his ass when he bends over to plug in the cord. His eyes meet mine before I can turn away and my face heats, yet again, in embarrassment. *Shit. He caught me checking him out. Will he kick me out? Will he be disgusted and angry?* Turning away from him and closing my eyes, I refuse to look at him again. I don't want to see the repulsion on his face.

Eleven

ALISTER

Chuckling at catching Ben staring at my ass, I head to the stove. It's obvious he doesn't have much, if any, experience in these types of situations, but it's an ego boost all the same. The moan that escaped his lips when he sat down had my dick hardening. It was the sexiest sound I've ever heard. Then to catch him checking out my ass when I was plugging in the laptop, I've had a semi since.

Cooking steak, potatoes, and green beans, I make sure he will get a good healthy meal full of protein and starch. I'll send leftovers home with him too, and make sure he eats tomorrow.

Making dinner, my mind wanders, taking in what I've just learned about the boy in my living room. I can't imagine what other necessities he lacks in his life. With no computer, he wouldn't have internet or cable either, two fewer bills he would have to pay. Does he have access to a phone, either a cell or a landline? From the hug I gave him at the college, I can tell he doesn't eat enough, and if he struggles to afford food, it's a good bet he struggles to pay for his rent and utilities.

He was afraid to enter my apartment because his boots were dirty, which tells me at some point he was probably beaten for tracking dirt into the house. You don't get that type of intense fear without a painful memory attached.

Hearing a pain filled groan, I glance into the living room to check on him. He's doubled over clutching his stomach, the laptop on the side table forgotten. Concern for him has me leaving the food, placing a hand on his back and kneeling next to him.

"Ben? What's wrong?"

His forehead is resting on his knees, and he's breathing erratically. He's obviously in pain, but I don't know why, where, or how to make it stop. It's a minute before he speaks to me. "Nothing, I'm fine." His voice is strangled, obviously not fine. I'm about to comment on it when I hear a loud growl from his abdomen, followed by a groan of pain. *He's hungry. Very, very hungry.*

"Hang on." Getting up, I hurry to the kitchen, and since the food isn't ready yet, I smear a thick layer of peanut butter on whole grain bread and hand it to him. Before I can even tell him to take it, he grabs it from me, folds it in half, and shoves half of it in his mouth. He barely chews before swallowing then finishes the bread.

"Dinner is almost done, are you okay for a few minutes or would you like another?" Squatting down next to him, I rub his back almost unconsciously, trying to comfort him. His breathing is still too fast, and his eyes are clenched tight, but the groaning has stopped. I get up to check on the food and make another piece of peanut butter bread for him, dropping down onto my haunches again. "Ben?"

He lifts his head when he smells the peanut butter. Not looking at me, he takes the offered bread and eats it slower this time.

"Ben, what can I do to help?" No one should be this hungry, ever. I can't imagine how it feels to literally be starving. His head lifts, his forehead shiny with sweat from pain, tears on his cheeks.

Hopelessness is clear in his eyes. I've never seen someone look so defeated. "Why me?" he whispers.

I don't have any answers for him, and I doubt platitudes will help. I hesitate for just a second before pulling him into me for a hug. It's all I've got. I can stuff him with food tonight, but I doubt I'll be able to charm my way into administration to find his address off campus.

Shifting to sit on the floor, I give him a gentle pull to encourage him to come to me. Ben climbs into my lap, arms around my neck, and his face in the crock of my neck. I can feel his tears as they hit my skin and soak into my shirt. My arms tighten around him, holding him securely. I want to protect him, soothe him. I wish I could tell him everything will be okay, but I don't know that. I don't know what his life has been like, what it will continue to be. The way he clings to me, I have a feeling he craves physical touch, who knows how long it's been since he's had a hug.

The front door opens behind me, which can only mean one thing, Alex is here. Ben tenses against me before quickly scooting off my lap, pulling his knees up to his chest and hiding his face.

"Ali! What's for dinner? Smells great man!" Alex's voice is hollering down the hallway. It's obvious when he's noticed I have a guest, and I can only imagine what the next words out of his mouth are going to be. "I knew you had a boyfriend, you lying son of a bitch." His laugh is carrying as he goes in search of food.

Taking a deep breath, I close my eyes for a second before focusing on Ben again. His arms tight around his legs, face buried behind his knees, he's preparing for an attack. I don't know if it's a verbal or physical attack, but he's preparing for either one, maybe even both.

"Alex, now is not a good time." Standing between Ben and my brother, I know he'll say something inappropriate, but he won't say anything hurtful. By the shit eating grin on his face, he's going to give me shit for this, get Mother in on it too.

"You're fucking a student, man! I knew you were more like me than you let on." He's so excited about what he thinks he's discovered, if only he could think with his brain for once. Pretending to wipe a tear from his eye, he says, "I'm so proud of you."

"Get out. Just get out." Taking a step forward I push him toward the door.

"Alright, alright, you're finally getting some action. I'm leaving. Watching my brother fuck some dude is not my idea of a good time."

"Get out!" I holler at him, pushing him again. The door is almost closed when his foot stops it so that he can get the last word.

"Don't do anything I wouldn't do." Then he all but cackles as he walks down the hallway. *Motherfucker.*

Taking a deep breath, I head back toward the living room. Ben hasn't moved from his curled up spot on the floor. I want to comfort him, but just then I smell something burning. "Shit!" Running into the kitchen, I turn all the burners off and quickly plate everything. The steaks are much more well done than I had intended, but they should still be edible. I get the plates set on the table, silverware, napkins, and glasses, before going back to him. Kneeling in front of Ben once again, I cup the back of his head, hating the way he flinches.

Rescue Me

I'm used to having to apologize for the crap Alex says, but this is different, I'm not sure what to apologize for. "I'm sorry about my brother. He's a horn dog, and he only ever thinks about his dick."

Lifting his head, his eyes find mine, his soul once again on display, crying out for comfort.

Twelve

BEN

I DON'T UNDERSTAND WHAT'S happened in the last hour. He invited me to his apartment and let me use his computer so that I could finish my homework. What teacher does that? He's fed me, comforted me, and hugged me. He's acting like he cares. Why? Is he trying to butter me up for something?

Looking up at him, even kneeling, he's taller than me. He put himself between his brother and me, protected me. No one has ever done that before. No one. I don't understand this guy. His brother showed up, and he didn't seem surprised I was here. He even joked about his brother fucking a student, a male student.

I realize he's been talking, but I haven't heard a word of it, lost in my head, thoughts reeling. "Why did he think I was your boyfriend?" The question flies out of my mouth. Why don't I have any control over the words oming out of my mouth around him? What the hell is wrong with me?

The crease between his eyebrows is back as he reads me. "It's kind of hard to explain."

"I'm sorry. It's none of my business." Lifting myself to sitting on the couch, I grab the laptop and try to bury myself in my homework, but the question keeps swirling in my head. *Does he have a boyfriend? Is his brother just messing with him, like it's a joke he's gay? Or is he into guys?*

He's still standing there, but for the first time, he seems unsure of himself. I'm not used to it, and it makes me uneasy. Closing the screen, I set it aside and stand. "I'll just go. I'm sorry for interrupting your night. Thank you for offering to let me work on my paper here. You have a really nice place." Leaning down to get my backpack, his hand settles on my waist as I stand, and my eyes jump to the warm milk chocolate of his.

"You don't have to go. Stay and finish your assignment, I made dinner, and there's more than enough for you." He lets out a breath that fans over my lips. "Please."

I can't take my eyes off his lips, he's tall enough that they sit right in my line of sight when I'm in looking at him. They look soft, warm, and sexy as hell. God, I want to know how they would feel pressed against mine. What type of kisser would he be? Would he be passive, letting me lead, or would he take control of the kiss? My dick is getting harder the longer I stand here, his hand still on me.

"Ben?" My name on his lips sends a shiver down my spine, forcing my eyes closed. When they open again, I'm looking into molten chocolate, and I'm closer to him than I remember being. Did I step closer or did he? I'm not sure, but I also don't care. My face is turned up to him, and he's leaning down toward me, his lips so close to mine. Lifting onto my toes, they almost meet, my eyes close in preparation for his lips to touch mine.

A cell phone rings, startling both of us. He clears his throat and steps back, shaking his head—*Son of a bitch!* Scrubbing my hands down my face, close my eyes and try to will the blood from my dick. I'm hard as steel, it fucking hurts.

"I'm sorry." Dropping my hands to my sides, Alister has both hands on his hips, and his head is dropped back on his shoulders, looking toward the ceiling. Dragging my eyes down his body, it's easy to see just how aroused he is. It's not just me feeling this pull, he is too, it's not one-sided. I don't know if that excites me or terrifies me more.

"I have to go," I say, reaching for my bag once again and swing it onto my shoulder.

"Wait, please. Have dinner, finish your homework. I'll go to my office and grade homework. I'll leave you alone. You don't need to be afraid of me."

He's pleading, asking me to stay. What does he want from me? He's always so confident, but not right now. Right now, he's unsure, pleading with *me*. I don't know how to handle this. I want to tell him it's okay, I'm fine. It would be a lie, since I'm not fine. I'm a fucking mess. I don't know what to do with the knowledge that my fantasy man wants me too. Does he actually want me, or has it been a while, like his brother said?

"Please." His whisper is once again a plea, his eyes begging me as hard as his words, and it breaks me. I can't say no to him.

"Okay." The word has barely left my lips when he smiles, his shoulders relax, and he lets out a breath. That damn smile chips away at the ice protecting my heart, weakening my defenses even more.

"There's a plate for you on the table, eat where ever you want, at the table or here in the living room. I'll take my plate and let you work." He turns and heads to do just as he said he would. I stand there, not saying anything or moving, just watching. Before heading down the hallway, he turns and smiles at me again. He is effectively shattering the wall protecting my battered and broken heart.

Thirteen

ALISTER

Goddamn it! Why did Alex have to come over tonight? Why didn't I message him and tell him? I almost kissed him. Ben. He's too fucking tempting. I didn't want him to leave without finishing his paper or eating a real meal. If I'm being honest, I don't want him to leave at all. I want him in my bed, pressed up against me. Sweaty and exhausted from a good cathartic fucking.

Raking my nails over my head, I push against my eyelids. I need to get a grip. I do NOT lust after students. I certainly don't kiss them in my living room. Fuck. Maybe I should have had Alex stay, act like a buffer between us. Pulling my phone from my pocket, I dial Alex and listen for him to answer.

"You're already done? I'm disappointed, brother."

"Shut up. I have a problem," I growl.

"Yeah, you got a hair trigger apparently. I don't know what to tell you about that. I've never had that problem." *Fucking hysterical.*

"Would you stop thinking with your dick for five damn minutes?"

"Damn, I'm just screwing with you. What's up, man?"

"I almost kissed him." Pacing across my bedroom, I'm going to wear a hole in the carpet.

"Almost?"

"Yes. Almost. He's my fucking student! He shouldn't be in my apartment to begin with, but I offered him a place to work when he got kicked out of the library."

"Wait a minute… he's really your student? I wasn't serious when I said it. What the hell are you doing?" I have his attention now.

"They physically threw him out of the library! He's got a paper or something due tonight and no computer at home, he was about ready to explode when I saw him. I offered to let him work on it here." Groaning, I'm in so much shit if anyone on campus finds out about this, I continue, "I don't know what it is about this guy, Alex."

"I know everyone at work thinks you're straight or a monk, but you've never done anything like this before. Don't let him go. Ali, don't let him go." I'm not sure I've ever heard him this serious before. It's not helping my heart rate, that's for damn sure.

"I could lose my job, my career, over this. I work at a Christian university. They will never tolerate a homosexual teacher, especially if they find me with a student."

"You'll find another job. There are a lot of schools that won't give a fuck who you stick your dick into as long as it's legal and consensual."

"He's afraid of me. I don't know what to do about it or how to change it." I don't know how to handle being unsure of myself. I've known who I was and what I was doing since I graduated high school. I hate these unsure, insecure feelings.

"That sounds like a conversation for Mom. Can you think of a way to get them to meet? I'm betting she would love to talk to him."

"He's afraid of getting the carpet dirty. He's literally starving. I want to help him, but I don't know how."

"Again, a conversation to have with Mom. I really don't care about a chick's back story as long as she's willing."

Making a disgusted sound in my throat, I can't imagine living my life that way, I say, "One day, a girl is going to come along and knock you on your ass. I can only hope I'm there to see it happen. You really are a pig."

Laughter fills the line. "Yeah, I am. But it sure is hella fun. Seriously though, take it slow, get to know him. Show him you don't mean him any harm. You know what they say about actions speaking louder than words. You're a good man. He'll see that."

"Wow. Thanks, man. Just for that, I'm going to give you a little piece of advice. You ready?"

He chuckles again. "Yeah, I'm listening."

"Don't get herpes." His laugh once again fills the line between us until he's coughing.

"That's good advice. I'll do my best. Text me later and let me know how it goes."

"Alright, later."

We say our goodbyes and hang up. I feel a bit calmer, but I will need to talk to my mother about this. She's been a child psychologist since before Alex and I were born, working with at-risk youth most of the time. She is the most amazing woman. If he's from around this area, there's a chance they've crossed paths. I'm not sure if that would be awesome or really weird. Probably both.

I haven't touched my food and it's more than likely cold by now anyway. I have to know if he's still here or if he ran the second my back was turned. I want him to be comfortable here, to be comfortable with me. I can't remember a time when it was important to me, when it was important for a specific person to be comfortable in my home, in my presence.

Opening the door quietly, I listen for any tell-tale sounds. Clicking of the keyboard or utensils on the plate, anything. I want him to eat and I need to know when he leaves here his stomach will be full and happy. Somehow, I need to make sure he leaves with leftovers but not make it seem like I pity him.

I can hear him typing on the laptop, so I know he hasn't left yet, deciding to fake needing to pee, I leave my room to check on him. Since the hallway is short, he can see me once I've stepped through the door. Like a deer in the headlights, he freezes, staring straight at me. I give him what I hope is a comforting smile and a nod before heading to the bathroom and closing the door. I feel like a teenager again, trying to sneak glances at a crush.

Turning the water on I go through the motions of having to pee, so I'm not in here for a weird amount of time. I have no idea how much attention he's going to pay to this little trip. After a minute, I flush and wash my hands then leave the confined space.

He hasn't moved at all since I stepped out of my room. "You doing alright? Need anything?"

He looks up over the computer and shakes his head. "I'm just sending the email to my teacher now."

I look at his plate and see he hasn't touched it. "That's great. I'll pack this up for you to take home." He looks like he wants to argue, but I pick up the plate and head to the kitchen before he gets a chance. He didn't touch it, and I don't understand why, he's obviously hungry. *Maybe he's embarrassed?*

Heading back to the living room, he's packing his stuff into his backpack, perfect timing. "Here you go." I smile when I hand it to him, acting like the situation is completely normal. He looks at it for only a second before taking it and adding it to his bag.

"Thank you."

"You're welcome. Do you need a ride?"

"No, but thanks, I'll catch the bus. I really appreciate you letting me work here. Thanks again."

"It was no trouble at all. I'm glad I was able to help."

We stand there in awkward silence for a minute before he swings his bag onto his shoulders. "Well, I need to get going to catch my bus."

Stepping back, I give him room to walk passed me. "I'll see you in class on Monday."

He nods at me then closes the door behind him.

See you in class on Monday? God, I'm an idiot.

Fourteen

BEN

Out of breath from running to catch the last bus, I drop into an empty seat and press my forehead against the glass. Tonight has been one of the strangest and most confusing nights of my life. I don't know what to think or how to feel. He almost kissed me. He cooked food for me, tried to make sure I was comfortable. Why would he do that for me? I'm a nobody.

My phone vibrates in my pocket, startling me from my thoughts. Without looking at the screen, I know it's Kristen.

"Hey, Kris, what's up?" I greet, my forehead still pressed against the glass.

"Where the hell have you been? I've been trying to get ahold of you for hours!" she yells.

"I'm sorry. I was working on homework."

"Bullshit. If you were working on homework, you would have told me. I've heard literally nothing from you for three hours!"

"I…" Taking a deep breath, I know the next words out of my mouth will bring a shit storm. "I was at Mr. Bennet's house."

Silence. Looking at the screen of my phone, I check to see if I dropped the call.

"Hello? Are you still there?" I ask.

"You were where?" she screams this time, and I'm forced to pull the phone from my ear.

"It's a weird story, and one I'm honestly not really sure about. But I ended up at his apartment working on homework."

"Oh no, you start from the beginning and tell me everything!"

Letting out a sigh, I tell her what happened, how I was thrown out of the library, how he hugged me and offered to let me work at his apartment, even how he cooked food for me. "That's it. I finished my outline, emailed it to my teacher, then left." My cheeks are hot from the lie of omission. There was so much more to it.

"Really? That's it?" She doesn't believe me.

"That's it," I tell her as I get off the bus and start the uphill climb to my so-called home.

"I don't believe you. You're a shitty liar, you always have been."

"What the hell gave me away?" I demand.

"Ha! That right there. You fall for it every time. Now spill the beans."

"He hugged me again, I wasn't feeling well, and he gave me some bread with peanut butter on it to help settle my stomach. I was so embarrassed. He kneeled in front of me and hugged me, pulled me into his lap."

"No, he didn't!" she gasps.

"Yeah, he did. I was in his lap when his brother showed up. He has a twin brother, they're almost identical, by the way."

"Wait! I knew he had a twin brother, but nowhere did I find that they were identical! There's two men who look like him?"

"The brother is just as buff as he is, but with tattoos. He's a horn dog though, according to Mr. Bennet."

"Damn. Anyway, go on. You're in his lap, brother shows up."

"I was scared whoever it was would attack me, you know? Being gay isn't the most accepted thing. So, I sat on the floor. Mr. Bennet stood in between us and kicked his brother out. The brother made a joke about having sex with a student and not wanting to see his brother fuck a dude."

"What? Is he gay? No one has *ever* seen him with *anyone*! Not even a rumor!"

"He is, at least, I'm pretty sure he is. After the brother left, I tried to leave. I screwed up his plans. I was just going to get going, but he stopped me, and he almost kissed me." My face heats again, thinking of how close he was, how amazing he smelled.

Finally getting to my building, I climb the steps to my floor, all the while listening to my best friend freak out. I smile for the first time today. I always feel better after talking to her, she has a way of making it seem like things aren't so bad or as confusing.

"What happened next? Why didn't he kiss you?" she demands.

Unlocking my door, I let myself in and lock the deadbolt behind me. "His phone made a noise, ruined the moment. Then he disappeared into a room to let me work."

"That's it? Nothing else happened?"

"Well, when I finished my outline, he came back into the living room and asked if I needed anything. I told him I was just going to send an email and I would be out of his hair. He made a point of looking at the plate he left for me on the table, then looked back at me. He told me if I didn't eat it, I had to take it home."

"I like him more and more all the time."

"Shut up. Anyway, I tried to argue, but he wasn't having any of it. So, my backpack has a full meal in it."

"I assume you haven't been eating again. How many times do I have to tell you I will gladly have groceries delivered? I'm happy to do it."

"You're not buying me groceries. I'm fine."

"If our situations were reversed, would you buy me groceries if I needed it? Or pay my rent? Or anything else?"

"Of course, but that's not the point."

"It's exactly the point! Why is it okay for you to pay for things for me but not the other way around?"

"How did we get on this topic? I'm not arguing with you about this again. I need to know what to do about my situation!" I lay the pity on a bit thick, but I really need her help here. "You know I have zero experience."

"I've never kissed one of my teachers, so how the hell should I know what to do?" Letting out a sigh, I lean back and lay on my sad excuse for a bed—damn it's freezing in here. "So, just go off of what he does?"

"That's probably the best. No one knows anything about his relationships on campus, so keep this close to your chest. Not that you're a blabbermouth or anything."

"Who would I tell? You're my only friend."

Fifteen

BEN

It's been almost a week since I was in his apartment and he almost kissed me. We haven't talked to each other since that night, which is probably for the best because I can't get him out of my head. My desire for him has only intensified, has me stirred up and crazed. Something has to give soon, or I will explode. Looking at the paper in my hand isn't helping.

I failed. The first big test of the term and I bombed, hard. Swallowing the lump in my throat, I shove the paper in my backpack so I don't have to stare at it any longer. My cheeks are hot with embarrassment and shame. I want to hit something, get into a fight to release some of the anger I have toward myself. I'm a failure. Dan told me that enough times that I should be used to it by now. I will end up sleeping on the damn street because I can't pass this stupid math class. I was born on the street, so I guess I'm destined to die there too.

The entire class I'm fuming in my shame—the unfairness of life. Nothing has come easy for me, I've had to fight for the right to survive since the day I was born. What made me think this was going to be any different? Maybe it's time to whore myself out, try to fuck Mr. Bennet so he gives me a good grade. I hear it works for girls and I've seen the way he watches me, he almost kissed me, he wants me. I could suck his dick if he gave me a C, just enough to pass so I can graduate.

The thought of having his dick in my mouth makes my dick twitch. I've never been with a man, but I've thought about it, fantasized about what it would be like to be taken and take in return. Mr. Bennet is always starring in my dreams and fantasies. Would he be a gentle lover, slow and careful? Or would he be hard, deep, and fast? Would he be demanding, growling orders at me, or would he be submissive and waiting for my orders? I don't know which I want more, for him to fuck me or for me to fuck him.

I'm rock hard, confined behind faded dark jeans while I wait for class to end and everyone to leave. I can't think past the blood pounding in my ears, my mind full of visions of Mr. Bennet taking me on his desk right here in the classroom.

Suddenly, everyone stands and collects their things before shuffling out of the room. A few students remain to ask him questions about the test. I don't know how he's so calm with them, but he never shows anything but patience. My eyes are glued to him, the way his muscles flex beneath his button-up shirt when he writes on the board. One by one, as he answers their questions, the students leave. It seems to take forever, but I'm finally alone in the room with him.

Tension fills the space between us, our eyes are locked on each other as we wait for the other to make the first move.

"Ben," Mr. Bennet starts. I can't stop the shudder at the way my name rolls off his tongue. A tongue I want to feel on every inch of my body. "I think a tutor is necessary in order for you to pass this class."

"You tutor me. I'll work around your teaching and office hours. I don't want to learn from anyone else, only you." My eyes are stuck on the bare skin showing through his open collar. *When did I get so bold? When did I become a predator stalking prey?*

I can hear his voice but can't understand the words over the blood pounding through my ears. Standing, I stride directly to him. When I'm in front of him, I look up into his eyes and put my hands on his chest.

His lips stop moving, and he sucks in a breath. Beneath my palms, his heart thunders, his breathing ragged. Leaning forward, I place a kiss on his breastbone, between his pectoral muscles. Goosebumps form under my lips and a shiver racks his body.

His hand pushes inside the hood of my sweater and grips my hair, bringing my mouth to his. Wrapping my arms around his waist, I cup his ass and bring his hips to mine. Fuck he's got an amazing ass, I've been dreaming of squeezing the firm muscles for months, so I let myself have this moment, grinding my hard-on against his. I can't count the number of times I've wanted this.

The groan rumbling in his chest vibrates my own, making my tip start to leak, damn near ready to explode. He spins us, pushing my back against the whiteboard, the pen tray digging into my lower back, but I don't care. Bending his knees, his free hand grips the back of my thigh, an encouragement to hook my leg around his hip. He's grinding against me, his cock against mine and it's taking all of my self-control not to cum in my jeans. My grip on his ass tightens as I struggle for control over my body as my fantasy comes true.

Ripping his mouth from mine his eyes are closed tight.

"We have to stop." His words are breathy as his forehead meets mine. "Anyone could come in and catch us." We're trembling and breathing hard, but have stopped grinding against each other, my thigh still being held in his hand.

Closing my eyes, I can't look at him. "I'm sorry, I shouldn't have touched you. I don't know what came over me." I'm embarrassed and more turned on than I have ever been, but I just molested my teacher.

He chuckles before I feel his lips on my forehead. "It's alright. I didn't mind."

Dropping my leg and taking a step back, my gaze is on the tile floor. "I know I need a tutor. Please help me. Please." I'm afraid to beg, but I'm more afraid of not passing this class and being homeless.

He's quiet for so long I'm afraid he won't respond.

"Okay," he whispers. My eyes snap to his, unsure I really heard him.

"Really? You'll tutor me?" I'm so relieved, I don't know what to do with myself. I want to hug him, but I'm afraid to touch him again.

"Send me an email with your class schedule, and we'll figure out a time. Sound good?" He's laughing at my excitement, the smile in his eyes is a dead giveaway, but I don't care, I have a chance of passing this damn class.

Sixteen

ALISTER

Watching Ben leave my classroom was harder than it should have been. While I enjoy checking out his ass, I wanted to be inside of it more. I still can't figure out what it is about him that has me so worked up, so possessive. I want him to be mine, I crave him, to kiss him, fuck him, sleep curled up with him. He's so broken, down to his soul, and I want to fix it.

Shaking my head, I grab my stack of papers and head back to my office. He does need help, since math is not his strong suit. I feel for him, I know I'm lucky in the sense that math has always come easily to me. Most college students live in fear of the math class they are required to take to graduate, but I took extra math classes as elective credits. If I didn't get at least a B+, I took the class again.

Unlocking my office, I lock the door behind me and keep the overhead light off to deter students from lining up outside and blocking the hallway. Starting a cup of coffee, the aroma fills the small space as I hit the voicemail button on my phone.

"Hello Alister, this is your Thursday reminder. See you at dinner! I hope you have a marvelous day and I can't wait to hear all about Ben!" Her voice makes me smile; I love that woman.

Thinking of Ben has the smile dropping from my face, what the hell am I going to do about him? I can't be caught dating a student. It'll be career over for me. And if anyone finds out I kissed him, it'll be just as bad. I'm sure my name will be drug through the mud. I never imagined having this kind of an issue when I accepted the job offer. I assumed I would meet a guy and fall in love slowly, giving me plenty of time to switch jobs before anything serious happened.

I rub my chest absently, the spot where Ben's lips touched my skin is tingling. I haven't spent much time alone with him, I barely know him, but I feel a need I've never felt before—a need to know him.

The drive to my parents' house is quick as my mind races in circles. The what-ifs making me crazy as the different outcomes swirl around. By the time I'm parking in the driveway, I'm frustrated and damn near ready for a fight—a rare state for me to be in.

Alex opens the door, standing with his arms crossed over his chest, that smug smile on his face. Right now, I hate seeing that stupid smile on my face looking back at me. A growl rumbles in my chest as I step on the porch and Alex raises an eyebrow at me.

"What's eating you?"

"None of your business," I snap, stepping around him. His laughter follows me into the house. Running on autopilot, I kiss my mother's cheek and say hello to my father. It's not until I'm standing in the kitchen that I realize I don't have flowers or beer. I've been so wrapped up in my head I forgot to get them on the way over. Closing my eyes, I suck in, and then release, a deep breath.

"I'm sorry Mother, I forgot your flowers."

"I don't just want you here for the flowers, Alister. I want to see my son," she informs me very matter-of-factly.

"Your boyfriend break-up with you?" Alex's voice comes from over my shoulder.

"I don't have a boyfriend. Drop it."

"Then who pissed in your coffee?"

"It's none of your damn business! I said, drop it!" It's been a long time since I've yelled, the last time was probably in this house when I was a teenager and full of testosterone and raging hormones.

Everyone stops what they're doing to look at me, but no one says a word. I can't take it, everyone expecting an explanation from me. Shoving against Alex, I stomp past him, heading down the hallway to my old bedroom. Slamming the door once I'm inside, I lay down on my old bed and stare at the ceiling. I know my mother will come up here in a few minutes to tell me I need to apologize for blowing up at my brother, who I'm lucky to have. She'll work some magic and get me to spill my guts, and I won't even realize it.

Right on cue, there's a knock on the door. "Come in," I holler, sitting up against the headboard. Mom walks in, closing the door softly behind her. She brushes at some invisible speck of dust before folding her hands in front of her and looking at me. Her face is carefully blank, no accusation or anger anywhere.

I sigh and drop my chin to my chest, and once again I'm fifteen. "I'm sorry."

"I'm not the one who deserves an apology."

"Yes, you do, I came in angry and looking for a fight. I had no right to come in here like that." When the bed dips, I look up to see her sitting.

"You won't ever have to apologize to me for having emotions, but you will have to apologize for not handling them well."

All I do is nod, I've heard this line about a thousand times in my lifetime.

"Are you going to tell me what has you so worked up, or are we going to dance around it all night?" She looks at me expectantly, but I know she will take me at my word if I tell her I don't want to talk to her about it. It's one of the reasons she's so easy to talk to. There's never any pressure to talk, but there is always an ear to listen.

"It's Ben." At my words, she nods, fully aware of where my issue is stemming from. "I don't know what to do about him."

"In a perfect world, what would you want to happen?"

"He would be mine. The university wouldn't care. I was with a man, a *former* student. I like my job, but I wish they were a little more open-minded, or at least didn't care so much. I would be able to date or marry anyone I wanted, and it would have zero effect on my employment." When I look at her again there is a knowing smile is on her face. "What?"

"So, if I understand you correctly, you're torn between exploring a relationship with Ben and your job?"

"In the simplest form, yes." *Why is she smiling? What has she figured out in five minutes I haven't been able to in weeks?*

"Tell me this, does your happiness depend on your current job or do you imagine you could be just as satisfied at another college?" She sounds like this is a very simple question, which the question itself is, but what does it have to do with anything?

"I'm sure I could be just as satisfied at a different location…"

"And do you think your current job will ever be accepting of a homosexual relationship?"

"No, I don't—" But she cuts me off before I can finish my sentence.

"Is your job worth your happiness?"

"Mom, what are you getting at? Just spit it out."

"Answer the question, is your job worth your happiness?"

"No! No job is worth anyone's happiness!" I shout, frustrated at the mind games she makes me play and frustrated when they work. "I hate it when you do that."

She's smiling again, a knowing smile that all mothers have when they know they've won. "If I had come in here, sat down, and said 'no job is worth your happiness,' you would have huffed at me, not believing it for a second. This way, you came to the same conclusion on your own, and you believe it."

Standing, she brushes her skirt, then opens the door. "I do believe you owe your brother an apology. You're lucky to have him, you know."

Shaking my head and following behind her. "I know, Mom."

Seventeen

BEN

***He kissed me. Alister** Bennet kissed me. He was hard for me…*

    Chewing on my bottom lip to hide the ridiculous smile on my face is going to leave me with a raw, painful lip, but I can't stop. Before getting on my bike to head home, I text Kristen saying we needed to talk as soon as I get to my apartment. I'm definitely not talking about this in public, no way in hell. Plus, it's hard to talk while on my bike.

    The ride is short, ten minutes at most, and I'm into my neighborhood. Since it's raining, my hood is pulled up, and my backpack is heavy tonight. I have a lot of studying to do this weekend. I don't have Friday classes this week, so I have three full days to devote to school work. It helps that I don't have a TV or computer to distract me either.

I get to the gloomy, rundown building I currently live in, with chunks of the concrete steps missing, and carry my bike up three flights of creaky stairs. The entire building is disgusting, probably ready to fall or go up in flames. Honestly, I'm surprised it hasn't been condemned. Finally getting to my apartment, I unlock the door, bring my bike inside and secure the door behind me. I drop my backpack on the floor and pull my phone out of my pocket to email Mr. Bennet my class schedule when the screen lights up with an incoming call from Kristen.

"Hey, bitch."

"Hey right back. Are you home? Can you talk?"

"Alister Bennet kissed me."

The line goes quiet for a second. It's not very often that I get to surprise her like this, and I am enjoying every second of it.

"What the hell did you just say? Because I know it wasn't Alister Bennet kissed you."

Falling back to lay on my bed, I laugh at her response. I love her so much. "That is, in fact, what I said."

"Bullshit!"

"No bulls were involved."

"Tell me everything! Where, what, when, why, and how?"

"Today started out shitty, all day I've been in a bad mood. He handed back our tests from last week, and I bombed it. I guess it was the final straw. Once everyone left the classroom, I asked him to tutor me. Okay, I basically demanded it."

"Wait. You demanded he tutor you?"

"Yeah, I really have no idea where that came from. Anyway, I walked up to him and kissed his chest."

"What the actual fuck? Who are you and what have you done with Ben?"

"Stop interrupting! He kissed me right after, like pushed me against the whiteboard, hand in my hair, wrapped my leg around his hip. I've never been so turned on in my life. I really thought I was going to blow a load in my pants. But he pulled back and had to be smart, said anyone could walk in and see us."

"I am so insanely jealous right now. Your day was way better than mine."

I laugh again, who needs therapy when you have a best friend who makes you laugh? "Trust me, before that my day was shit."

"Hang on a damn second. Are you saying I never turned you on? We dated for almost four years."

"Sorry to break it to you, but vaginas do nothing for me."

She fakes outrage by sucking in a loud breath. "So, you used me? How could you do such a thing to little innocent me?"

"Ha! Innocent my ass. You corrupted me, slut."

She starts laughing. "You're damn right I did. Someone had to."

"You'll forever be my one and only straight fuck though." My voice sounding reminiscent.

"You'll forever be my gay lover. Which is a good thing 'cause boy, you don't know what to do with a vagina. At. All."

"Are you serious right now? I had *zero* experience! I bet I could rock that shit now."

"Yeah? Been playing with a lot of vaginas since I transferred?"

"No, but I know the power of Google. And porn."

We both crack up laughing before ending our phone call. I lay there smiling like a loon, while I type out my email to Mr. Bennet. Kristen is the only person I've ever been able to feel free around, like I don't have to pretend or hold back. I hope someday I can find a man to be with that I can feel equally as comfortable around.

I send the email and sit up, my stomach growling in hunger, but since I haven't gotten my financial aid check, I have no food. Great. Another long night of hunger pains.

Eighteen

ALISTER

After dinner Thursday night, I've thought a lot about what my mother tricked me into figuring out, no job is worth my happiness. Seattle is the land of advanced education, and you can't go anywhere without seeing a college or university. There has to be a better fit for me, a place that is more accepting.

It's been a while since I went for a good hike and before the weather turns nasty, I want to go up Mount Si one more time. Grabbing my phone, I flip to Alex and send him a message.

Ali: You off today?

Alex: Yeah, why? Boyfriend leave you hanging?

Ali: Hike Mount Si today?

Alex: Are you trying to kill me?

Ali: Ha! Lazy hike today, no trail running.

Alex: Fine. You talked me into it. Pick you up in 20.

Grabbing my hiking gear, I lay it all out on my bed before grabbing a quick shower. Forcing myself to keep on track, and not get distracted by thoughts of Ben, I'm out and dressed in record time. By the time Alex walks in my front door, I've checked the weather forecast, packed my backpack with all necessary items, and have laced up my boots.

"Alright princess, your chariot awaits." Alex's tone is deadpan.

Rolling my eyes, I swing my backpack over my shoulder, and we head out of the door, locking it behind us.

"What happened to your boyfriend?" His signature smirk is back in place.

"I don't have a boyfriend," I say, again, as we climb into his SUV. Since he has a four-wheel drive, we take his car instead of mine when we go on hikes. My car would get stuck with the least amount of weather.

"How's it going with the kid from your apartment?"

"I don't know."

"Oh, come on. I've known you since the moment we developed brains, I know you've got something figured out."

I know when it comes down to it, I can trust him, but at what point will he take it seriously and not crack jokes? I know I'm not doing anything illegal, lusting after a student goes against the code of conduct for the University, but it's not going to get me arrested.

"Honestly, I don't really know much." Turning my head to look out the window as the buildings become a forest. "I can't quite figure him out. Sometimes he's shy, withdrawn, and seems terrified of everything. Other times, he's full of sarcasm and anger, he gets almost an aggressive streak."

The car quiets as we both think about what I've just said. It's not an uncomfortable silence at all, there is no one I'm more comfortable with than my brother. He truly is so much more than just a brother, he's my best friend, sounding board, the comedic relief when life gets too serious, and my accomplice when I was young and prone to doing dumb shit.

"Sounds like a defense mechanism, he was probably abused, maybe even still is." Alex has a lot more experience in this area than I do, being a Seattle police officer. Having a child psychologist as a mother definitely influenced his career path, while I took after Dad with my love of math.

"What's your train of thought there?"

"Well, he's typically quiet, doesn't want to draw attention to himself, probably scared of his own shadow because life has taught him people will hurt him. When he gets into a situation where he feels in danger, he tries to brush the conflict away or downplay it by being sarcastic. Once he's been pushed too far, things build up, and he gets angry or aggressive."

We drop into silence again, his explanation swirling through my head. The need to protect Ben flairs in my chest. While I'm tutoring him, I'll get to know him, build trust, and hopefully, he'll let me help him.

"Alright, grab your shit and let's get this thing started. I got a hot date tonight." Alex wags his eyebrows at me as he climbs out. Sometimes even I'm surprised by how different we are. We look almost identical, but our personalities are very different, he's always joking around, a man whore, and straight, and I am the complete opposite.

Grabbing my backpack, I pull my beanie on, and we head to the mouth of the trail. This is one of our favorite mountain trails, it's an intense hike, but the views are amazing when you get to the top. Most of the trail is covered by a canopy of forty-foot trees, so even in the rain it's not too bad, ferns and moss are everywhere, bringing a lush green to the forest floor.

We're about a quarter of the way up the three and a half-mile climb when we stop for a water break.

"So, who's the lucky girl?"

That knowing smirk appears on his face immediately. "This gorgeous little blonde chick I met at the gym, Jill. She's smoking hot."

"I'll take your word for it."

He laughs at my deadpan response. "She's got a great ass."

"Okay, now you've got me, I do appreciate a nice ass. Though I don't find most women's asses to be that great looking."

"How are we even related?"

"I don't know, but Mom swears we shared a womb."

Putting the water bottles back in our bags, we continue the climb. The mountain is quiet, peaceful. And I don't have to hear my brother talk about his sexual adventures.

Since we're taking our time, not battling to beat each other to the top like normal, it takes us three and a half hours to get to the peak. When we break through the tree line, it's all jagged rock, but the view below is breathtaking. Finding our way to a big flat bolder, we sit down and unpack our lunch, and luckily it's not wet today. After the climb up, we're half starved. We don't take time to talk or even to breathe much as we inhale our food.

"Alright, let's get back down. I need to shower before I meet Jill." Alex slaps my leg before standing and heading back to the trail. Shaking my head, I follow him. I love this mountain trail, and I hike it more than any other in our area. The climb is difficult, steep, but only takes a few hours. With the difficulty of the hike, there isn't much chance to talk, since there's slippery spots to watch out for.

At the trailhead once again, heading toward the SUV, we're tired and sweaty, but satisfied with the workout we got today. My phone vibrates in my pocket, letting me know I have a notification. I always turn my sound off while hiking, as I don't want the sounds to disturb the quiet peace of the forest.

Alex unlocks the doors, and we toss our packs inside before sliding into the front seats. Pulling my phone out of my pocket, I check my notifications and see Ben has emailed me his class schedule. It looks like his weekends are clear, maybe he can get together tonight.

I type out a quick reply, asking him if he wants to meet up tonight and where the best place is for him to focus, and rest my head against the back of the seat. Anticipation is making it harder to relax, something I'm sure Alex notices.

"Seems I'm not the only one with a hot date tonight." He smirks at me.

"It's a study session. He desperately needs a tutor."

He starts to chuckle, and I know exactly what's about to come out of his mouth.

"I knew you were just as dirty as I am. Get that young ass."

"Seriously? How old are you?"

"Three minutes older than you, my brother."

Ignoring Alex, I wait for a reply from Ben.

Nineteen

BEN

MY PHONE PINGS, THE 4G holding long enough to let me know I have a new email. The only time I get emails is if someone wants money or junk mail, but since I just sent Mr. Bennet an email, I take the risk and look. *Holy fuck he wrote me back already. And he wants to meet tonight.*

Stunned, I panic and freeze. What do I do? Do I meet up with him tonight? Where would I meet up with him? He can't come here. Absolutely not. He probably suggested meeting up somewhere to avoid having me in his house…

Flipping to Kristin's contact information, I call her. She'll know what to do. With every ring, my anxiety increases. Her voicemail picks up, and I end the call. *Fuck.*

I need a shower.

What do I wear?
Where do we meet up?

Thinking it over for a second, I send him the address of a pool hall I use to hide out at while I was a teenager. I still stop in and say hi to the owners, Trish and Jason. It's always been a safe place for me. Hell, I even slept there a few times. I'm comfortable there, he won't stick out too much, and I've done homework there countless times.

A few emails back and forth and we nail down a time to meet. Grabbing a quick, freezing shower, I dress in the best clothes I can find, and head down to catch the bus.

Arriving at Ball Scratcher's Pool Hall, I make my way to the office, sure Trish will be hard at work. Knocking on the door, I wait.

"Come in!" she calls out in her sweet voice. Opening the door, I step inside and wait for her to notice me.

"Ben!" Her face lights up when she sees me, jumping from her chair she wraps her arms around me in a tight hug. "I'm so glad to see you." I hug her back just as tightly. She really is the nicest person I've ever met. She never asked many questions when I would come here, but she could tell I didn't have a good home life so she would feed me and let me crash on the couch in the breakroom when I needed it. I would help her clean up after closing.

"I'm glad to see you too." Stepping back, she surveys me. "Do you mind if I take over my normal table? I'm meeting someone to study with."

"Of course! You're welcome anytime, you know that." She smiles at me again and cups my cheek. What I wouldn't give to have had a mother like her. Closing my eyes for a minute, I soak in the comfort of her touch. "Thank you."

"No need for thanks. Make sure you stop by the counter and say hi to Jason."

"I definitely will." I give her another hug and let her get back to work. At the counter I wait for Jason to be done with a customer, before stepping forward for him to see me.

"Ben! I thought I recognized you. How are you doing?" Jason comes around the end of the counter to give me a hug and a slap on the back.

"I'm doing okay, thanks. I'm in my last term before graduating." A fact I'm damn proud of.

"That's great! I always knew you were meant for more than hanging around here."

I'm about to respond when the bell on the door signals someone entering. Turning toward the sound, I get a few seconds to look at Alister as he takes in his surroundings. The black and white tile on the floor is chipped in spots, it's seen better days. The walls are a bit dingy with dated pictures of people and dogs playing pool. It reminds me of a bowling alley but with pool tables instead of lanes.

His eyes sweep the area and zero in on me, locking his gaze with mine as he walks over, taking me in, my blood heats as if I can feel the caress. My face flushes when Jason clears his throat next to me.

"Oh sorry, Jason, this is my teacher, Mr. Bennet. Mr. Bennet this is an old friend, Jason." I can't meet either man's gaze.

"Mr. Bennet, welcome. If you need anything, please don't hesitate to let me know." They shake hands while I pretend not to exist. Why did I think this place was a good idea? I have too much history here. He must think I'm a loser.

"Call me Alister, please. And thank you, Jason, that's very kind of you." Turning to me, he says, "Hi Ben, shall we get started?"

I nod and without saying a word, lead us to the table tucked away in a corner in the back of the room. This was where I always sat, there was no way to sneak up on me, and it's close enough to the kitchen to make a quick getaway if I needed one.

Looking at the table, I realize I never checked to make sure this is okay with him. "Is this okay? It's where I normally sit," I mumble, turning toward him.

He steps closer to me and lays his hand on my back, the warmth seeping through my sweater. "Perfect."

Pulling out chairs next to each other, we both sit, and I pull out my textbook and notes. Looking at Alister, I notice a smirk is on his lips. "What?"

"You're getting right to work. I like that you're taking this seriously."

Embarrassment heats my cheeks again, and I turn my head to stare at the table. "I know you don't have to help me. I appreciate it and don't want to waste your time."

"I am happy to help you, Ben. I want you to pass." He dips his head to try to make eye contact with me. He scoots his chair closer, his arm brushing mine on the table as he opens the book. "Okay, let's get started…"

He flips through my notes and homework, finding where I started to struggle, and starts his lesson there. It's so hard to concentrate when he's this close to me, and I find my eyes trained on his lips more often that I would like. Shaking my head, I force myself to look at the paper where he's writing out equations and explaining the steps, explaining why things have to go in a certain order.

It's starting to click an hour later, my brain hurts, but I'm starting to get it. Alister writes out an equation for me to solve and hugs me to his side when I do it correctly without his help. Reacting on instinct, I turn into him, my face in the crook of his neck and my hand on his thigh.

Blood rushes to my dick, desire and uncertainty fighting for the next move. "Ben," his voice is rough as his hand covers mine. "Maybe we should take a break for a bit."

Rejected, I sit up in my seat. "Do you want to play pool? I'm not very good, but we can play if you want."

"That sounds like a great idea. Excuse me for a moment, I need to use the restroom."

I head to the counter for balls as he heads to the bathroom. This time, Trish is working the counter while Jason cooks. "Hey Ben, what can I get for you?"

"Can I get a set ball, please?"

"Of course, honey, here ya go," she offers, handing me the balls. I thank her and head back to the pool table closest to the table we were working at. I rack the set while trying not to watch Alister walk toward me, but my eyes gravitate toward the confident stride he has. He owns any room he walks into, his presence felt by everyone, and I am damn sure not immune.

With everything set, I grab a cue and chalk the end, hoping he wants to break since I've never been very good at it. Alister grabs a cue. "May I borrow your chalk?"

Handing the cube over to him, our fingers touch and electricity shoots through me, stealing my breath for a moment. The smirk that forms on his lips tells me he felt it too, and he liked it.

"Do you want to break, or shall I?" he asks, heading for the head of the table.

"Go ahead. I've never been very good at it anyway." A hum is the only response I get as he leans over the table to set up his shot. The snug fit of his shirt shows the movement of his muscles when he stretches to brace his hand on the felt. Blood roars in my ears and gathers in my jeans, suddenly making them much tighter than I remember them being. I'm standing at the opposite end of the table, watching his every move. His hand pulls the cue back to strike, and his eyes flick up to meet mine when he shoots.

My body is about to explode. I can't move while he walks around the table toward me, that smirk still on his lips. My eyes are locked on his. "It's your turn, I'm solids." His voice rumbles in his chest.

Pulling my eyes away from the temptation in front of me, I look at the table. Balls are scattered everywhere, and nothing looks like an easy shot. Moving around to get a better angle, I lean over and shoot my cue at the white ball. The ball hops and jumps off the table, rolling under a nearby chair—*son of a bitch*.

My face is hot with embarrassment. This was a terrible idea. I need to get my stuff and go home to lick my wounds. Hopefully, he won't ever bring this up again.

Twenty

ALISTER

Grabbing the ball, I walk back to the table to stand directly in front of Ben. He looks mortified, but he won't look past my collarbone. I place the ball back on the felt and face him with only a few inches separating us.

"You don't have to put on a show for me, I want to get to know the real you." His eyes are glued to the exposed skin at my neck, he licks his lips, and a moan passes my lips involuntarily. "You can't look at me like that." My voice is low and rough, like sandpaper against delicate skin.

With one hip against the table, I place my hand on his hip and lift his chin with my fingers. I need to see his eyes, see if he's as affected by me as I am by him.

"Like what?" His voice is a whisper against my lips. I lean in, inhaling his scent and stroking his cheek with mine, my hand running along his jaw and into his hair.

"Like you can already feel me," I say against his ear. I'm painfully hard, ready to explode when he shutters against me. Before I realize what I'm doing, I have him sitting on the pool table with me standing between his thighs. I cover his lips with mine, using my hand in his hair to angle him just the way I want. My lips steal his moan when he opens for me.

Pressing my body against him, my tongue runs along his lower lip, sucking on the plump flesh. He moans again, wrapping his arms around my neck and leaning into me. His dick is hard against mine, and it takes every ounce of self-restraint I possess not to strip him naked and fuck him over this table.

I pull my lips off his, panting harshly as I take a look around the room. My eyes collide with a woman behind the counter, her knowing smile lighting up her face. *Shit.*

Ben doesn't loosen his grip around my neck and uses the advantage to drag his teeth down my jawline to my ear, which he sucks between his teeth. It's my turn for a shudder to course through me, my cock is hard as stone and ready to blow. Turning my head back to him, I lay my forehead against his with my hand still in his hair, praying he stops kissing me before I lose control.

"Ben," my voice cracks, "come home with me."

Shocked, he pulls back to look me in the eye. Emotions shoot across his eyes, surprise, want, fear. "Please." I'm so close to begging, I want him in my house, in my bed. I can tell he isn't experienced, I would never push him to do anything more than he is comfortable with, but I want my sheets to smell like him. I want to be wrapped around him, cocooned in warmth and comfort.

"Why?"

His question surprises me. Every reason is so fucking obvious to me. Is he questioning my morals, wondering if

I'm just in it for a quick fuck, or does he not see what is happening here?

"Because..." I struggle to find the right words. "Because I want to get to know you better, the real you, not just as a student. Because I can't seem to keep my hands or my lips off you and this isn't the place for it. Because... because no matter how hard I try, I can't get you out of my head." I let out a deep breath, hoping my words have comforted him instead of scared him. His eyes are roaming my face, I let the heat and need I feel for him show on my face, not hiding behind the teacher mask I'm so damn good at wearing.

It feels like an eternity, but he finally nods his head. A smile breaks out on my face, and I can feel it to the tips of my toes. I lean in and place a soft kiss on his lips before backing away, giving him room to get down.

"Do you want to play first?" I ask, since we had just started the game.

"Uh, not really. I think you've seen the extent of my abilities." His sarcasm makes me chuckle, he's never shown me this side of him—the side with humor and sass. Gathering his things, he shoves it all into his backpack and swings it over his shoulder.

"I just have to say goodbye, and then we can go." He's self-conscious again, looking at the ground instead of me. I don't know what happened all of a sudden, but I'm intrigued.

"No problem. Take your time." I follow his lead to the counter and stay a few steps behind to give him some privacy. The woman that saw us kissing comes out from behind and gives him a long tight hug, like a mother who hasn't seen her child in ages. They speak quietly for a moment before she cups his cheeks and kisses his forehead.

Turning to the kitchen, she hollers, "Jason! Ben is leaving!" The large man with greying, brown hair that I saw at the counter earlier comes from the back, wiping his hands on a towel. He's taller than me with a pot belly and an easy smile. The elevated floor of the check-in counter distorting his size and appearance. Even though he's large, he doesn't feel intimidating at all. Jason wraps his arm around Ben's neck and pulls him in for a hug, including a slap on the back. "Take care, don't be a stranger."

I can't see or hear Ben's reply, but he steps back toward me and motions to the door. He's embarrassed about knowing these people, but I don't understand why. Are they relatives? Does he think I would look down on people who work at a pool hall? Making our way to my car, our silence isn't exactly comforting, but I let it go until we're driving.

"They seemed to know you pretty well," I comment, breaking the silence.

"Yeah, I've known them a long time." He's turned away from me, watching out his window.

"Are they relatives? Aunt and Uncle?"

"No, just friends." He obviously doesn't want to talk about it, so I stop pushing him for answers. "I've been going there since I was a kid. I lived not too far from here." His voice surprises me.

"They've been working there that long?"

"They own it, Trish and Jason. They're really good people." He goes quiet again. I have a lot of questions, but I don't want to sound like I'm interrogating him. "They sometimes take in the unwanted youth off the streets, give them a warm place to sleep, food, and all they ask for is some help cleaning up."

Unwanted youth?

"Mmm," is my only response. I don't want to break the spell of him opening up to me, but my heart breaks for him. I can't begin to understand what his life has been like. Unwanted youth on the street? I know all too well some of the horror's kids go through since my mother works with kids, but I've never come face-to-face with it.

"I don't know what I would have done in the winter without them." His voice sounds far away, like he's no longer here with me. Moving slowly as not to startle him, I place my hand on his leg and give it a light squeeze. He shakes his head and looks down at my hand for a moment before resting his hand on top. "Sorry."

"You have nothing to be sorry about."

"I didn't mean to bring the mood down."

Giving his leg a little shake to get his attention, I pull into my parking spot and turn to face him. "Knowing your past was hard doesn't change the fact that I want to know it. And I started it. I asked about Trish and Jason." With a half-smile and a nod, we get out of the car and walk side-by-side to the elevator. The doors slide open and close softly, Ben is fidgeting, picking at his fingers, so I take one in my hand, interlacing our fingers.

"Are you okay?" I ask.

He nods and clears his throat.

"Nothing has to happen. We can just talk, watch a movie, whatever you want. No pressure." His head turns to look at me as the doors open. Pulling him along with me, I unlock my door and don't give him time to think about the carpet before closing the door behind him.

Twenty-One

BEN

THE DOOR CLOSES BEHIND me. My stomach is in knots, I'm so damn nervous, but I'm also excited. I want to be here. I want to be with Alister. He makes me feel good, normal. I'm once again in his apartment, but the reasoning is so different this time. We're standing in the entryway, staring at each other. Suddenly, he seems unsure. *Does he regret asking me to come here?*

"Are you hungry? Thirsty?" he asks, still holding my hand.

"Sure." *Maybe he just needs something to do?*

He leads us into the kitchen and grabs a beer to offer to me. "No thanks, I'm not much of a drinker. Water would be good." He hands me a water bottle and grabs one for himself. I watch as he twists the cap off and chugs half the bottle, the muscles in his throat working, my feet glued to the floor. He catches me staring and lowers the bottle, setting it on the counter.

"Why don't we have a seat in the living room? We can talk or watch a movie or something."

"Okay." My voice is soft. I hate being so unsure of myself all the fucking time. I really am a waste of space.

Alister leads the way to the living room, with me following along behind him like a lost puppy—the analogy not far from reality. He sits on one side of the couch and looks up at me. Sliding my backpack off, I sit in the recliner next to the couch.

He smiles like he can read my thoughts as easily as he reads a book. "Why don't you come sit next to me?" My cheeks heat from embarrassment yet again.

The lights are low in here, just the entryway and kitchen lights are on. This feels serious, intimate, and though I'm trembling, I move to sit next to him. I'm rewarded with a smile that relaxes some of my nerves.

"You don't need to be nervous around me." Alister has turned sideways in his seat to face me and I mirror his position.

"Am I that obvious?"

He chuckles and lays his hand over mine. "Yeah, it's pretty obvious, but I have a theory about it."

"A theory about me being a scared little girl?"

He laughs again, I'm really starting to like that sound. "Not a scared little girl, but perhaps, inexperienced?"

"That bad of a kisser, am I?"

"Not at all, in fact, I would say you're one of the best kissers I've locked lips with."

Embarrassed again, I don't know what to say. I've already made an ass out of myself, so I might as well keep going. "Who knew straight girls were good kissing teachers?"

"Wait, what?" He's chuckling again.

"I'm sure you've discovered my childhood wasn't lived in Disneyland. My best friend helped keep me from being bullied. Not only at school, but at home and we had to make it look real." I shrug my shoulders, trying to play it off as not a big deal.

"That's some friend."

"She is my best friend to this day. She's going to lose her mind when I tell her about this." I instantly regret my words. Now he knows I'm going to talk about him, that he's a big deal to me. *Shit.*

"Hey, don't clam up on me now. I was just getting you to relax."

Closing my eyes and shaking my head, I let out a sigh. "I don't know how to do this."

"Do what?"

"This. Talk to people. Have friends or relationships."

"Have you ever had a relationship? One that didn't involve kissing a straight girl?" I appreciate his attempt to lighten the mood.

"No."

"Ben. Look at me, please?" Both of his hands are on my knees, the heat of his palms pressing into my cold skin through my ripped jeans. I lift my head to look at him, not sure what I'm going to find but hoping it's not soul-crushing.

"I'm not sure why, but I like it. I'm the only man to know what your lips feel like, to know the sounds you make when you're turned on." I cover his hands with mine and move his hands up my thighs, forcing him to lean in closer. He shifts to come into my space, a smirk on his face. "Do you want me to kiss you?"

"Yes." The word barely leaves my lips when I press them against his. He shifts again, and I lay down, Alister coming over the top of me. I've always wondered what this would feel like, having a man pressing into me, his weight against me. *It's fucking magic.*

I move my legs, and his hips rest against mine, his cock rubbing against me. I'm already on edge and ready to cum. He rips his lips from mine and buries his face into my neck, still moving against me.

"Fuck. Tell me to stop."

"No, don't stop. Please don't stop."

A guttural moan emanates from his chest and it pushes me over the edge. My feet hook over his ass and pull him down harder on me as I moan, cum filling my underwear. My hands are fisted in his shirt, painfully tight, but it isn't until my orgasm is over and all my bones turn to liquid that I notice it.

He drops on me, completely relaxed but breathing hard, he came hard too. The knowledge that I made him cum is exhilarating—giving me just a little self-confidence boost.

"We should clean up." His voice is muffled by the couch cushion, which makes me laugh. This is not the best time to laugh, I know it's not, but I can't stop it. Alister lifts his head and looks at me with amusement. "Something funny, Mr. Wallace?"

"Nope. Not at all, Professor Bennet."

"Touché."

Sitting back on his knees, he helps me up and kisses me softly.

"You can use the hall bathroom. I have a master. Washcloths are under the sink."

Twenty-Two

ALISTER

IN THE MASTER BATHROOM, I strip off my pants and boxer briefs before wetting a washcloth in the sink. I have cum drying on my leg, sticking to the hair, but it doesn't bother me. I'm the first man to kiss Ben. I've never felt possessive over a man, but I know I will fight tooth and nail for him.

It takes a minute, but I get cleaned up, and as I'm pulling on clean underwear, I hear my front door open and close. *What the fuck?* Quickly getting to my bedroom door, I rip it open and see the back of my brother opening the guest bathroom.

"Alexander! Get the fuck out!" I holler, stomping down the hallway.

Spinning around, he looks like he's seen a ghost. "I didn't know! I'm sorry! I didn't mean to see your boyfriend's dick!" His hands are up in surrender, but since he's in his Seattle PD uniform, it's not very believable.

Grabbing the bathroom doorknob, I slam it closed and push Alex out of the hallway. "I swear to God Alex, you gotta start knocking. I'm going to start deadbolting the door. What the hell are you doing here anyway? I thought you had a date?"

"I did have a date, and then these jackasses decided to call me in. I need to pee!" he yells, sprinting for my bedroom.

Leaving my brother to take a piss, I go to the bathroom door in the hallway. I don't know what to say. This isn't exactly a normal situation. "Ben?"

I sigh and lean my forehead against the door. "I'm sorry. My brother and I need to set up some new rules." I'm met with silence. I don't know if he's embarrassed beyond words, terrified and huddled in a ball on the floor, but I need him to answer me.

Alex appears at the end of the hallway, looking guilty for the first time in his life. "I'm sorry man. I was on patrol in the neighborhood and needed to take a leak."

I nod, accepting the apology without a second thought. There's no way Alex could have known Ben was here, but that's exactly why I'm going to need to start locking the door when he is. I have a feeling Ben will need the extra second of warning to prepare himself mentally.

Alex leaves, shutting the front door behind him. I'm still stuck in the damn hallway, not knowing what to do about Ben. My knuckles tap against the door. "Please talk to me." I'm leaning against the doorjamb, one hand on either side when it cracks open. A haunted, black iris peers at me. I know I need to step carefully here, he's skittish and needs reassurance.

"Hey, you okay?" I keep my voice soft, non-threatening.

The door opens farther, and I can see most of him, his clothes are straightened. His eyes travel down my body and stop at my hip, dropping my gaze to see what has his attention, I realize I'm standing here with no pants on.

I let out a little chuckle. "Oops. Why don't you come sit on the couch while I grab some pants? I'll be there in just a second. Okay?"

"Okay." His words are soft as I lean in to kiss his forehead, before heading back to my room for some lounge pants and a t-shirt. When I get back to the living room, Ben is zipping up his backpack and I assume he was putting his underwear inside. He's sitting on one side of the couch, so I sit on the other side and turn to face him.

"I'm sorry." His words catch me off guard.

"What do you have to be sorry for?"

"Your brother knows what we were doing. I should have been faster or locked the door. It's my fault." The words rush from his mouth, he really is afraid I'm angry, that I blame him.

I scoot closer to him, laying my hand over his. "My family knows I'm gay."

Ben's fingers stop fidgeting, and confusion has his eyebrows pushing together. He looks up at me, still confused. "They do?"

"Yeah, I came out to my family a really long time ago."

"And they're okay with it?"

"Yes. My family doesn't care. If I like guys, girls, both, to dress up as a pony, it doesn't matter to them. I promise you have nothing to fear from Alex."

He thinks about it, absorbs the information, before nodding. "Okay."

"Are you hungry? I can whip us up something to eat." At the mention of food, his stomach growls. "Well,

I guess that answers that," I say with a chuckle. "Come on, keep me company in the kitchen."

I take his hand and thread our fingers together. I love the way our hands fit, the way his face lights up with a smile. I lead us to the kitchen, leaving him to settle against the cabinets while I look in the fridge. "Shrimp fried rice?" I ask, looking over my shoulder at him.

He shrugs. "I'll eat anything. I'm not picky."

"A man who's easy to please, I like it." I wink at him. All the supplies are set on the counter, and I get to cooking. I get my love of it from my mom.

"Is it weird if I ask about classes?" I ask him.

"Seems like it should be, right?" I look over at him and he's sitting on the counter, looking relaxed and sexy, hair ruffled. He catches me staring and blushes, a smile tugging at his lips.

"You don't have to be shy around me. I like your sarcasm and wit."

"I'm trying." His gaze is holding mine.

"Good." I turn back to the stove and stir the rice, season it as I need to. "So, what are you going to school for?"

"It's pretty boring."

"I'm a math teacher. I think I can handle boring."

His chuckle makes my heart sing. "Organizational Leadership. Basically, how to be a boss."

"Yeah? You wanna be a *boss*, son?"

He laughs, head back against the cabinet door. He looks so much younger when he laughs—light-hearted, mischief lightening his eyes. I need to see more of him like this. With the stove turned off, I dish us both up some food and lean my lower back against the counter across from him.

"You have a great laugh," I comment, scooping food into my mouth. A light blush colors his cheeks, and it's damn adorable. I want to touch him again. Like a kid with a new toy, I want to play with him. He scoops a spoonful of fried rice into his mouth and groans, the sound has my blood pounding through my body.

"This is so good," he says around a mouthful of food.

I chuckle, I seem to do it a lot around him. "I'm glad you like it. I can teach you how to make it yourself if you'd like."

His eyes meet mine, surprised and excited. "Really? No one has ever taught me how to cook." I can feel the smile covering my face, reaching my eyes.

"That settles it then. I'll teach you how to cook anything you want. If I don't know how, we'll try it for the first time together."

"I would like that. Thank you." I wink at him again, resuming the shoveling of food into my mouth. His spoon clatters in his bowl when he sets it down.

"Damn, you must have been starving." He shrugs his shoulders and looks uncomfortable. Placing my bowl on the counter, I step toward him, invading his space. "I'm glad you're here."

The smile he gives me is everything. In this moment, there's no pain or fear, just contentment and happiness. With a smile on my lips, I lean in toward him, leaving just a breath of space between us, hoping he'll make the first contact this time. My eyes are at half mast, watching him. He looks at my lips, sucking on his own, but shifts his eyes to mine when I stop and wait. With our eyes locked on each other, he closes the gap between us. Hands appear on my waist, fingers flexing. "If you want something, take it," I say against his lips, wanting him to explore me, get comfortable with touching me.

My hands stay on the counter next to Ben's hips. I want to touch him, but I know I need to take this one step at a time. I can be patient, wait my turn to touch. The hands on my waist move to lift my t-shirt, his cool fingers brushing along my abdomen. The temperature of his skin and the exploration of his fingers has goosebumps breaking out along my flesh. I follow his lead, letting him take the kiss wherever he wants it to go, light and playful, passionate and full of sex, whatever he wants.

We stay in the kitchen, making out and exploring for a long time. When he pulls back, I kiss his forehead and take a step back. "Up for watching a movie?"

"Yeah, sounds good." He grabs his water and takes a long pull, sliding off the counter. I catch his hand in mine again and lead us to the couch. I lay down against the armrest with one foot on the floor and one on the cushion, then pull him down to lay against me. He's tense, stiff, but once I wrap my arm around him to rest my hand on his chest, he relaxes into me. Grabbing the remote, I flip through the movies on my Apple TV and select The Greatest Showman. It's not hard to watch Hugh Jackman and Zac Efron dancing and singing, plus the message of the movie is amazing.

We settle in to watch the movie. I pull the blanket off the back of the couch and cover us. In no time at all, Ben's asleep. Snuggling down to lay my head against the armrest, I give into the comfort and fall asleep too.

Twenty-Three

BEN

I'M SO WARM. I *must be dreaming, my apartment is never this warm in the winter. Maybe it's on fire.*

Laying on my side, I slowly gain awareness. There's someone behind me with an arm around my waist, their chest and hips are against my back and ass. *Did I fall asleep at Alister's?* I pry my eyelids open and look around the room. I'm definitely still at Alister's.

Butterflies erupt in my stomach, a smile taking over my face. He's the most amazing person I've ever met. Not only is he sexier than should be legal, but he also has an amazing heart, he's patient. And for some unknown reason, he wants me. I have nothing to offer him, but I want to. I want to be important to him and I want to be his.

The arm under my neck moves and Alister's breathing changes as he wakes. I hold as still as I can, not sure what to do now. The arm around me moves, flattens against my lower stomach. The muscles tighten with excitement and anticipation when his hand slides under my t-shirt, stroking my skin. My breathing increases, and my blood is pounding so loudly it's all I can hear while it pools in my morning wood. Soft bristles of his close-cropped beard tickle my neck, his teeth nipping where neck becomes shoulder.

I can't stop from arching my neck to give him better access. I never want him to stop. My ass pushes into his hips, the soft fabric of his lounge pants doing nothing to hide the raging hard-on inside. His lips don't leave my skin as he explores every inch he can reach, all the while his hand is moving up my chest to pinch and pull my nipples, and scratch at the hard muscles of my stomach. My hips are moving on their own accord, trying to thrust into something, anything, that will lessen the pressure.

A whimper sounds, taking me a minute to realize it was from me. Alister stops moving, the hand that was exploring my chest now holding my hips still. I'm panting, desperate for anything and everything.

"Fuck. I'm sorry." The rasp of his voice full of lust, sending a shiver down my spine. "I normally have better control over myself."

"That's okay," I get out between breaths, trying to force my heartbeat to slow.

His forehead rests against my shoulder, his breathing is just as rapid as mine. "It's not okay because I don't want to push you." He starts to sit up, so I move to give him room and sit up myself. Not sure why he stopped or what he means, I keep my hands to myself and my head down. My stomach is in knots again, and I don't know what to do or say, what the normal protocol is.

"Hey," Alister says next to me, reaching for one of my hands in my lap. "It's not your fault I seem to be a horny teenager when you're around."

"Okay," is all I can think to say. It may not be my fault, but I don't know what to do about it either.

"Come on. Let's get some coffee." He stands and pulls me up behind me. In the kitchen I stay out of his way by keeping close to the doorway. He turns on the Keurig and grabs two mugs. "How do you take it?"

"I don't drink coffee." Embarrassment is heating my cheeks. I can't afford a caffeine addiction, especially if it means needing milk and sugar.

"Oh, okay. Tea?" He's looking at me, trying to read me. I'm sure he can see the blush on my face, the uncertainty I'm trying so damn hard to hide. Once again, the walls I've built crumble at his feet, leaving me vulnerable and pathetic.

All I can manage is a shake of my head, looking at the tile beneath my feet, hands in my pockets. I shouldn't be here. I don't deserve to be here. Alister is so much better than me, deserves someone better.

Turning from the kitchen, I head for my backpack and swing it over my shoulder.

"Ben?" Alister is calling me, but I ignore him, I never should have come here. "Ben." The way he says my name has goosebumps covering my skin. I'm almost to the door when his hand on my arm stops me. I don't turn to look at him, I need to leave, but if I look at him, he'll convince me to stay. I'm on a one-way road to getting my heart put in a blender.

He walks around me and slides the hand on my arm down to hold my hand, interlocking our fingers. I love when he does that.

"Hey, what just happened? I offered you coffee, and you stormed off."

"I shouldn't be here. I need to head home. I have studying to do before Monday. Thanks for last night, it was… amazing…" I'm staring at his chest, the rise and fall of his breathing.

"If you want to go, I won't stop you. You're free to leave whenever you'd like." He still has my hand, but he steps aside, giving me access to the door. I take a step toward it when he speaks again. "I know you don't have much experience with dating and getting to know someone romantically, so if you need space, that's not a problem. I'm happy to take this as fast or slow as you want, I just need you to communicate with me. I'm not a mind reader, only a math teacher." I smirk at his joke, breaking some of the tension I feel. "As for last night, you are more than welcome." A pull on my hand has me locking eyes with him. "I'm happy to repeat the performance anytime." A smug, knowing smirk lifts one side of his mouth. I desperately want to kiss him again.

When he let me have control last night in the kitchen, it was heady, intoxicating. I felt powerful for the first time in my life, even if it was only for a few minutes and because he gave it to me. No one has ever given me power, I'm always forced to give away mine.

As badly as I want to stay, I know I need to leave. It's late enough in the morning that buses are running so getting home won't be an issue. I should have enough money left on my Orca transit card that I shouldn't have to walk. "I should head home."

He nods, smiling when I tell him what I need. "Okay, let me know when you get home?"

"Sure." I'm staring at his lips. I want to feel them against mine again.

"Ben?" When I hear my name, I realize he's said it more than once.

"Yes?"

"I'm going to tell you the same thing that I told you last night, if you want something, take it." His chin lifts in challenge, and I know he caught me watching his lips. Reaching up and cupping the back of his neck, I lift, crushing my lips to his. I can feel his smile for only a minute before his need to kiss me back takes over. Both of my arms wrap around his neck, lining our chest up to press together. A groan vibrates my chest, and I don't know if it was him or me, it doesn't matter. We stand in the entryway, mouths to hips locked together, fighting our desires for more.

The kiss continues, nips, sucks, licks, until I'm backed against the wall, my thigh held in his strong hand. Flashbacks to his classroom, when I was angry and frustrated, replay in my head. My hips grind against his, aching to feel the same pleasure he gave me last night again. Alister rips his lips from mine but doesn't drop my leg. "Do you know how badly I wanted to fuck you over my desk that day?" he pants, breathing heavily.

"You did?" Butterflies in my stomach have reached an all-time high, their wings dancing along my insides, and fire licks at my veins.

"I could picture it, shoving everything off the top, bending you over it. I struggled the rest of the day to get the image out of my head." Lust has his voice dropping an octave, low enough to feel.

"Holy fuck."

Alister chuckles, teeth dragging against my neck. "If you want to leave, you should go now, before we cross the point of no return."

My heart is pounding like it always does around him, and I'm gulping in air like I just ran a marathon. I can't think past my pants, the lust and arousal currently rampaging through me. I close my eyes to think, forcing my eyes off the temptation pressed against me. *Leave. I need to leave.*

"Okay, I'm leaving." Even to my own ears, I don't sound sure, but it needs to happen.

"Do you want me to drive you home?" The second the words leave his mouth, my stomach plummets. He can't ever come into my neighborhood. He will stick out like a sore thumb, and someone will jump him. I can't let that happen.

"It's okay. I'll take the bus. No need for you to drive me." I hope I sound more relaxed than I feel. I don't want him to know where I live. It's dangerous. Full of druggies willing to do anything for their next fix, thugs trying to make themselves feel better and make a quick buck—definitely not a place for Alister.

He takes a step back, unwrapping himself from around me, and I can tell he sees right through my bullshit. "I don't care where you live, but if you prefer for me not to know, that's fine. For now." His arms circle me, holding me like I matter, like he actually cares. I hold him just as tightly. "I want to know everything there is to know about you. I'll show you that you can trust me." He squeezes me again, kisses my forehead, then steps to the door.

Twenty-Four

ALISTER

When the door shuts behind Ben, I have to force myself not to go after him. I know it's ridiculous to want him with me constantly, we need time apart to process what is happening. Especially him. Everything about this is different for me, but he's never been in a romantic relationship with a man. A lot of men try to be "normal" before realizing that women just don't do it for them. Hell, even I did.

Sitting on the couch, I drop my head back and stare at the ceiling, replaying the memory.

On the back deck with Alex and our girlfriends, Jessica and Amber, taking a much-needed food break after swimming and screwing around in an above ground pool my parents put up. The summer sun is heating our skin and drying the girls' long hair. Mom made sandwiches and a fruit salad, and the girls eat like civilized humans, while Alex and I shovel food into our mouths as fast as we can.

Alex finishes his plate and grabs Amber around the waist, lifting her onto his lap and kisses her shoulder. I watch them unabashedly as they enjoy the closeness. I don't think I've ever felt that way about Jessica. She's a nice girl, smart, pretty, but I don't ever find myself just wanting to touch her, not like Alex does with Amber. I give her hugs, hold her hand, and kiss her sometimes— it's not like I find her repulsive.

We chug some water and throw our plates away before getting back in the water. We're splashing around and laughing when the guys from down the street come running out of our house, pulling shirts off and kicking shoes into the air. We're all friends, we hang out and play sports together, we've grown up together. Seeing them without shirts on is not new or unexpected, it's almost a daily occurrence. More and more over the last few years, it's harder not to watch them, but today, I can't turn my eyes away. Hard chests and flat abdomens, lean muscle covering bodies just starting to turn from boys to men. I have to lean into the side of the pool to hide my erection, the last thing I need is for anyone to think I'm gay.

Once the guys are in the water, and my issue has gone away, at least to a passible level, I join in the fun of wrestling, splashing, and general roughhousing.

"Alister." My dad's voice has me turning to see him standing on the deck. "Come inside for a second." He turns and heads back in, knowing I'll do as he's asked of me. I always do.

I hop over the side, grab my towel, and head into the kitchen where my dad is sitting at the breakfast bar. "Yeah, Dad?"

"Have a seat."

Wrapping the towel around my hips, I sit on the barstool and wait. It's only when something serious is happening that Dad talks to us one on one without Mom, and typically, it has to do with sex or something else guy related.

"How are things going with Jessica?" He looks relaxed, taking a drink of the dark beer in his glass.

"Uh, fine I guess." I really hope this isn't another sex talk.

"You like her? You have feelings for her?"

"I dunno, I guess so." I shrug my shoulders.

"You guess so? It should be a pretty simple yes or no."

"We're not having sex if that's what you're getting at." I'm getting uncomfortable with this conversation and just want it to end.

"Do you want to? Have sex with Jessica, I mean."

"Dad. Come on." I roll my eyes and stand up to leave.

"You're sixteen. It's completely normal to want to have sex with every girl that walks past you."

A sinking feeling settles into my gut. Does he know? "Did you have this conversation with Alex too?"

"No, I didn't need to."

"Why not?"

"Because I can tell he wants to have sex with every girl that walks past him."

"I have a girlfriend." My response is lame, and I know it.

"Yes, you do, but I don't think it's what you want." He knows. He has to. I can feel the blood drain from my face and my heart pound in my chest.

I have no response. All I can do is stand there and stare at him, lost, angry, and confused. "I see the way you look at Jessica or don't look at her. I also see how you look at your teammates, your friends." He stands up too, putting us eye-to-eye. I shake my head, I'm not gay, I can't be. Alex isn't, and we're twins, we're the same. Dad wraps his arms around me and hugs me tight, one hand on the back of my head. "It's okay. It's okay if you like boys. It's okay to be gay." I shake my head harder and shove away from him, angry. "I'm not gay!" My outburst echoes in the kitchen before I storm upstairs and slam my bedroom door.

I lay in my bed for the rest of the day. I didn't even eat dinner. Ignored everyone that came to my door, even locked it to keep Mom and Alex out. My computer stayed off, and I refused to talk to anyone. A few days after that conversation, I broke it off with Jessica and felt lighter, and it was only about a month later when I came out to Mom. By the end of the summer, Dad and Alex knew too. Though Alex was pissed to be the last one that I told, his initial response was typical, "About damn time, man."

The memories have me thinking about Ben, wondering if he ever had someone to come out to. Did he have anyone that supported him, told him it was alright? Gave him a hug?

Twenty-Five

BEN

I HAD TO WAIT a while for my bus, but it gave me time to process. Taking in the city life around me, I realize I don't belong here. Women going out of their way to not walk next to me, elderly folk side-eyeing me like I'm about to rob them. I don't know if I can ever come back here and Alister can never come to my part of town. We can never work, not really, we're from two different worlds.

Getting on the bus, I sit with my head against the glass, watching the city change from thriving to dying. My stop comes up, and I exit, hood over my head, eyes down, as I walk to my dilapidated building. After spending the night in Alister's house, the differences between his building and mine couldn't be any more apparent. Where his building smelled clean and fresh, mine smells like mold and mildew. His has light colored walls and an elevator, while I have dirty, stained brown walls and stairs that are literally rotting.

The door to my apartment is so old that a good push with your shoulder would probably break it, the doorframe would splinter without much effort. I don't know why I bother to lock it. There's nothing inside anyone would want anyway. Pushing the squeaky door open and locking it behind me, I plug in my phone and wait for it to power on. I'm sure Kristen killed it last night by calling a hundred times.

The neighbors start fighting, again. Yelling, crying, screaming, and things being thrown. I sigh, dropping my head to my hands. This is where I belong, the life I'm destined to live.

My phone starts vibrating like crazy, all the notifications coming through from Kristen. I fell asleep earlier than I expected, but I was so comfortable laying against Alister. I was warm, my belly full, semi-relaxed from cumming, then my eyes closed and I got the best sleep I can ever remember having. Even my subconscious relaxed around him, and no nightmares plagued me.

Finally, my phone quiets, so I pick it up to wade through the notifications. Kristen's incessant text messages, voicemails, and missed calls has a small smile forming on my lips. I don't bother to listen or read any of them and just call her instead. It rings twice before her voice fills the line.

"Benjamin Robert Wallace, where the fuck have you been? I've been trying to get a hold of you for over twelve hours! Twelve!"

"I know, I'm sorry. I didn't mean to make you worry." I take a deep breath, knowing the shit storm that is about to hit me. "I was with Alister. I just got home."

"Excuse me? You were with Alister Bennet all night?"

"Yup. All night. We slept on his couch." Being careful of the charging cord, I lay back on my bed and sling my arm over my eyes.

"Wait. Back the hell up, you were at his house?"

I sigh, knowing I need to start at the beginning. "Okay, here's the whole story. Keep your mouth shut until I'm done. No interruptions. Got it?"

"Got it."

"Yesterday, he emailed me and asked if I was available to meet up to study. I picked the pool hall that we use to hang out at for him to meet me at. We studied for a while then he decided we needed a break, and I suggested we play pool." Her cackling laugh fills my ear. "Shut up. Anyway, that was a disaster. He kissed me, hard. Like lifted me onto the pool table and kissed the shit out of me."

"Oh baby, pool is the sexiest thing in the entire world."

"I said no interruptions. When he stopped kissing me, he asked me to come home with him."

"No shit? Go, Ben!"

"Shut it! So, I did. Go home with him. We made out on the couch, and in his kitchen, he feeds me, then we laid down on the couch and passed out."

"Does he know I'm the only person you've kissed?"

"Yes. I told him straight girls are pretty good kissing teachers."

"When are you going to see him again?"

"Probably in class on Monday because I will have to see him every time I go…"

She scoffs at me. "No, smart-ass. You know what I mean."

I don't answer right away, the truth is, I don't think I'm going to. It'll be better for both of us if I don't. He can move past whatever it is that makes him want to see me, and I can move on too. "I don't think I'm going to."

"What? Why the hell not?"

"Come on, don't play dumb."

"I'm not playing dumb. A smart, successful, incredibly attractive man wants to spend time with you. What's your problem?"

"My problem? He has no business being with me. He can have his pick of men, and he can find a better match than me."

"That's bullshit, and you know it."

"I do not know it. My apartment building smells like mold and mildew, some stairs and floorboards are literally rotting, and most of the time I go hungry because I can't afford food. He can do a hell of a lot better than me!" Now I'm sitting up and yelling, my arms waving around as I shout at my best and only friend.

"What? Why didn't you tell me it was that bad? I would have helped you! I can pay for an apartment with solid floors and food. Jesus Christ, Ben."

"I don't want your help, Kris. I don't want to be indebted to anyone when I'm done with school. If that means skipping a few meals and living in a shit heap, so be it."

"Where you're living is dangerous. Lord only knows what crap you're breathing in, not to mention the high probability of physical injury with rotting floorboards. You need to live somewhere better."

"It's fine. I'm almost done with school. I need to get some studying done. I'll call you later."

"I know you're blowing me off, but I'm going to let you do it anyway. You are worthy of more than you think. I love you."

"I love you too." We end the call, and I fall back onto my bed again. Mentally exhausted. I catch a scent of Alister and bury my nose in the hood of my sweater, inhaling deeply. His spicy scent sending my heart into a frenzy. I want to save it forever. Sitting up, I pull my sweatshirt over my head, so I don't rub his smell off the fabric. I set it aside on the bed and strip off the rest of my clothes to get into the shower.

By the time I leave the shower, my teeth are chattering, and my skin is turning blue. I swear the water is only a few degrees above freezing, but I'm clean. I pull on the warmest clothes I can find and crawl into bed, snuggling the sweater to my chest so I can fall asleep with the scents of nutmeg and coffee swirling in my head.

Twenty-Six

ALISTER

With the exception of the very first day of teaching, I don't think I've ever anticipated a Monday as much as today. I haven't heard from Ben all weekend and my mind has been running wild. I sent him an email since I don't have his phone number, but he never responded, I don't even know if he got home okay.

This morning I shoved a protein bar in my bag for later and didn't bother to brew a cup of coffee. I took a shower, got dressed, and walked to campus, because I was too anxious to sit around and wait. The rain is coming down hard today, so the mats inside the door are already soaked, "caution: wet floor" cones are set up, and it's only 8am. Inside my office, I let out a deep breath and turn on the Keurig, more from force of habit than from actually wanting a cup.

Sitting at my desk, my leg is bouncing, I've started five different things, but nothing is holding my attention. I've never been this distracted, this emotionally invested in anyone. I've spent so little time with him that it doesn't make sense, I shouldn't care this much, I shouldn't need him this much.

I can't sit anymore, pacing my small office only gets me more aggravated. Ripping open the door to stalk the halls, I'm stopped short. Without a word, I grip the back of his neck in my hand and pull him into my office and find his lips with mine. Frustration, irritation, and want turns the kiss more aggressive, but he doesn't back down. He not only takes my assault but gives it back just as hard. My entire body is hard, tense.

Backing up, my legs hit the small love seat and I sit, dragging Ben into my lap, refusing to break the connection. He doesn't hesitate to straddle my thighs, riding my hips like he was born to. One hand tangles in his hair, the silky strands are so damn soft. The other hand wraps around his hip to cup his ass, encouraging him. Ben is grinding against me with everything he has, the friction of jean on jean making us hotter. His mouth explores me, bites and licks, kisses and sucks, he's driving me insane. He grabs a fistful of my hair and pulls my head back, exposing my neck and latching on. I know he's going to leave a mark, I should tell him to stop, but fuck if I want to. I want his mark on my skin, his claim. I know the halls will be full of co-eds whispering about who did it, I'll be watched even closer for clues. His teeth bite into my skin and my breathing stutters.

I reach for his pants, wanting to feel him in my hand, wanting to make him feel good. The button opens, and the suction on my neck is gone. My eyes meet his, the endless midnight of his eyes are molten when I free his cock from the confines of his pants. The hard velvet of his most sensitive flesh in the palm of my hand. He's a bit longer than me but not quite as thick, and overall, it's a glorious cock.

His hands drop to my chest, his eyes on my hands, watching me pump and cup him. He shudders and groans, precum beading on his tip. My thumb swipes over the bead, and I bring it to my lips, his eyes following the movement. When salty musk explodes on my tongue, we both moan.

"Take my cock out." I barely recognize my voice, the deep command to it. He doesn't hesitate, his hands immediately moving to the buckle of my pants. It only takes a few seconds for him to have his hand inside my pants, grasping my cock. "*Fuck...*"

Ben's fingers are cold on my overheated flesh, but it feels amazing pumping my length. Moans, groans, and growls fill the small space around us, neither one caring about the possibility of being heard.

My hand works him faster, squeezing a little harder, twisting my fist around him. His eyes close and his head drops, leaning into the hand still on my chest. "Kiss me. Kiss me while you cum." I aim his dick toward my shirt, knowing I have another one in here somewhere. His mouth fuses to mine, his tongue mimicking sex has me ready to blow. My body tenses further, my cock grows bigger, and I shudder my release onto my own stomach, spilling over his hand. My release sets off Ben's, his whimpers caught by my mouth still sealed to his, as hot cum trails down my hand and pools on my shirt. I couldn't be more satisfied in this moment.

He shivers and kisses me softly before sitting back on my legs, careful not to make a bigger mess. Ben's body is completely relaxed, spent, and my chest fills with pride. I did that to him.

With a smirk on my lips, I chuckle. "Thanks for dropping by."

He smiles and stands up, tucking himself away, and grabbing the box of tissues from my desk to help me clean up some. With the worst of it taken care of, he helps me to unbutton my shirt, his eyes so intense I can almost feel it. The shirt is carefully folded and shoved into my bag.

Standing in my office shirtless, my hands on my hips, I look over at Ben to see him lost in his own head. Staring but not seeing. With fingers under his chin, I bring his lips to mine once again, soft brushes of skin against skin. This kiss is comforting instead of full of lust and need. His palm cups my prickly cheek, and turning my head, I kiss his hand then his forehead, before stepping back to dig in my desk for a shirt.

Ben's eyes zero in on my neck, leaving me to believe the mark is worse than he meant for it to be. "I hope you have a turtle neck in here."

I laugh at his response. I don't think I've ever had a hickey and I sure as shit don't regret this one. "Nah, I'll wear it with pride."

"I'm really sorry. I didn't know it would be that bad." When I glance up, he looks a little pale.

"Hey, look at me." I wait until he's not just looking, but seeing me, before I speak again. "I'm not sorry. Plus, I'm pretty sure it's a first for me, because I don't remember getting a hickey before."

Some of the color is back in his cheeks, but he still looks worried, maybe because I haven't seen it yet. Grabbing my phone, I turn the camera on to face me and take a look at the mark on my neck. It's red, almost purple, and looking at it turns me on again. My eyes meet his, lust meets fear. Seeing just how scared he is kills the buzz in my veins.

"Really, it's fine. I like it even."

"I think I should change classes," he blurts out, taking me by surprise.

"What? Why? Are you uncomfortable in my class because of this?" My hands motioning between us.

"I think it'll be better if you aren't my teacher anymore." He's looking at the floor again, backing toward the door. "I'm sorry." The door opens, and he's gone before I can wrap my head around what he just said. By the time the message gets to my feet to move, he's long gone out of the building.

What the fuck just happened?

The pressure on my chest is heavy, as I drop my ass onto the chair I was sitting on only a few moments ago. My mind runs wild, replaying every second we've spent together since we met a month ago. *Did I push him too far, too fast? Is he scared? Is there something I overlooked?*

Why does my heart feel heavy when I've known him such a short time?

Twenty-Seven

BEN

OUTSIDE OF THE MATHEMATICS building, my back hits the wall, and I slide down to curl into a ball. I did what I had to do. I did this to protect him. He can't be caught with me, it will ruin his career, and I am definitely not worth it.

With my head on my knees and my arms wrapped around myself, I let the tears fall. I'm weak. I'm nothing.

For a few hours, I let myself believe Alister cared about me. I felt safe and wanted as if he wanted to take care of me. It's pathetic how a few hours of peace can rip your heart out when they're gone. All weekend I talked myself into ending this before class, thinking his office would afford us privacy but not the comfort of being at his house. I kept my distance, didn't respond to his email, even though every fiber of my being wanted to. I wanted to see him again, be held again. It's better this way because he can find someone worthy of his time now.

Once the tears dry, my heart heavy and cracking, I sit in the dirt. Being up against the building means this patch is dry, and the bushes hide me well enough from people passing by that no one should bother me. It's cold out here, but nothing I've not lived through before, it's not even the coldest I've experienced. My phone vibrates, and I know it's Kristen, checking in on me again. I've been distant all weekend and haven't told her why. I know she'll try to convince me I'm wrong and I need to stay strong in order to get through it.

Digging into my pocket, I pull the phone out and see an email from Alister. My heart constricts, terrified of what it says. I stare at it for a long while before working up the courage to read it.

Ben,

I would really like to talk to you about this morning. I'm sorry I pushed you to do anything you weren't comfortable with, my emotions got the better of me. I know it's a terrible excuse, but it's the truth. The last thing I want is for you to be afraid of me or uncomfortable in my presence. With it being so late in the quarter, I don't believe you can switch classes. Please continue to come to class. I promise to be on my best behavior. I don't want you to fail your last quarter before graduation because of me. I'm happy to continue to tutor you as well or help you find someone else. Please don't throw away your future.

Alister

He thinks I'm angry at him? He did nothing wrong, everything was, in fact, perfect, I re-read the words, hearing his voice in my head, smelling his spicy scent, before getting up and heading to class. His class. I'll sit in the very back, not make eye contact, and be the first one out of the classroom when it's over. He's right about one thing, I can't let this ruin my future, no matter how bad it hurts.

I make sure to arrive with everyone else to blend in with the crowd. It's easy to get lost in a group of college students in morning classes because no one looks awake yet. The class begins like every other, with attendance being taken. However, when he gets to my name, there's a slight pause and tensing of his shoulders before he says it.

"Here."

He appears to breathe easier, knowing I'm not avoiding his class to spite myself. Once attendance is taken and homework is passed forward, Alister jumps into today's lesson, spending most of the hour with his back to the class. I can't say I blame him, I wouldn't want to look at me either if I were him.

The class drags with me spending more time staring at his ass than on the board. The girls are all whispering about the hickey, which is on full display, his black V-neck t-shirt doing nothing to cover it. I don't know if I should be horrified or proud of it, but my heart is in my stomach, so it doesn't matter.

The lesson finally comes to an end, and he turns to face the class, his eyes lingering on me for only a few seconds before asking if anyone has any questions. A few people raise their hands, and he goes over each question thoroughly, as he always does, then excuses the class. The entire time I'm packing up I can feel his eyes on me. I feel everyone's eyes on me like they can all tell it was me who left the mark on the teacher they lust after. I need to get out of here, off campus so that I can think again.

Stomping my way down the hallway, I head to the bike rack where mine is locked up, only to find a tire missing.

"Son of a bitch!" My outburst has birds taking to the sky in alarm. "Come on!" I kick the bike storm off to the bus stop. *Could today get any worse?*

Twenty-Eight

ALISTER

All day I have barely held it together. The bruise on my neck is sore and throbs when I move my head the wrong way. Every time it happens, I'm reminded of how I got it, of who gave it to me. A shiver runs down my spine, goosebumps break out along my skin, and the fist around my heart contracts.

Nausea cramps my stomach, my head pounds with caffeine withdrawal since I haven't had any coffee today. How can Ben have this strong of an effect on me? It's ridiculous, but he does. I need him in my life, and I need to know he's okay. In my office, I pull up the student information I have for him, name and email address. Since I can't access any of his other information, I pull up Facebook and search. After an hour of stalking every Ben or Benjamin Wallace I can find, I come up with nothing. What college student doesn't have a Facebook account?

With a growl of frustration, I turn off my computer and head home. The walk will help clear my head, and I can go down to the apartment gym to work off any lingering frustration.

The wind turns the rain into biting pellets against all exposed skin, which makes me think of Ben riding home on his bike. He only had a sweatshirt this morning. I hope he was able to stay dry and warm on his way home.

Twenty-Nine

BEN

STOMPING DOWN THE SIDEWALK after walking home in the pouring rain, I'm cold, wet, and pissed off. Who steals a damn bike tire? I'm fucked, I can't afford to replace it, so I either have to walk back and forth every day or find a way to pay for the bus ride.

Water squishes out of my shoes with every step I take, and shivers rack my body against the cold. Thoughts of being wrapped in Alister's arms plague my mind, and the warmth, both physical and emotional, that comes with being around him. My soul is weary, tired of pain and loneliness and never being enough. Just once, I want to be enough.

Climbing the steps of my rickety building, avoiding the soft spots, I make it to my door, but something isn't right. There's water on the floor in the hallway and it's coming from my apartment. *Come on! Why can't I ever catch a fucking break?*

The key unlocks the door, and I push it open to find my place flooded. There's at least an inch of water throughout the apartment, all my stuff is soaked, and there's a hole in the ceiling where water is pouring in. I don't own much more than the clothes on my back. I can probably fit everything into two garbage bags. Now I have to find a way to get it all out of here, heavy with water, figure out how to get it cleaned and dried before mold and mildew sets in, then find somewhere to go. I obviously can't stay here, I doubt the owners will fix the hole, and I know they won't replace my stuff. I have no money for a hotel room because my bank account has $2.48 in it.

Dropping down to sit on my waterlogged mattress, I drop my head into my hands and cry. *What have I done to deserve this? Why am I being punished? Did my mother know I was cursed, is that why she left me to die?*

I don't know what to do. I can't take any more hits. My phone rings in my backpack, reminding me there's still shit that needs to be done, like homework. Careful to keep my bag out of the water, I find my phone and see a message from Kristin to call her. Not having anything else to do, I call her and try to get a hold of myself before she answers.

"Hey, Ben!" She's having a good day, she either got an assignment she's excited about, or she just found some juicy information to write.

"Hey." My voice scratches my throat.

"What's wrong?" Instantly she can tell I'm not okay.

"My apartment is flooded. Everything I own is soaked, and someone stole my fucking bike tire." I hope I don't sound as hopeless as I feel.

"What is your landlord doing about the water? Do you need money for a hotel for a few days until it gets fixed?"

"I don't know how to tell you this, but I guarantee the owner isn't going to fix this. I'm fucked. The building is going to be condemned if this is reported to the city."

"What are you talking about? Of course, it'll get fixed. They are legally responsible for the building. If they don't fix it, they'll get sued."

"Kris, listen very closely, I live in a shit hole. No one in this place can afford to sue the owner." Frustration at my situation is bleeding through to her, and it's not fair. Sucking in a deep breath, I hold it for a minute to calm down.

"I don't know what to say to you, Ben. I've offered to help you numerous times, and you refuse to accept it. I don't know if you're too stubborn or just too stupid, but when you're ready, you know where to find me." The call ends, and I'm left alone with my thoughts once again. I've pushed the only person in my life away. I have literally no one.

Gathering the few clothes I own, I pile them on the bed, along with the few possessions I have. Digging into mostly empty cabinets, I find some grocery bags and start wringing out my clothes before placing them in the bags. School books are added to my backpack, along with any papers I can salvage. Looking through my stuff, I find some mostly dry socks and my boots to change into, they'll be better than my drenched converse.

Looking around, my entire life is packed into one backpack and a handful of grocery bags. What a pathetic existence I have. With one last deep breath, I glance around before leaving my key on the kitchen counter and closing the door behind me. I won't be back, there's nothing left for me here.

Once again, I'm off into the unknown, hoping I come out on the other side or freeze to death in my sleep. *Is this really a better existence than being at Dan's?* The sun set a few hours ago, turning the chilly night bitter and biting.

The temperature is not low enough to freeze, but not by much. Without much thought in my direction, I start walking. At some point, I hope to find a covered bench or mostly empty overpass I can hide from the wind and rain for the night. I'm homeless. Hopeless. Lost.

I don't know how long I've been walking, but I can't feel my fingers anymore, I can't feel most of my body because of the cold. A car pulls up next to the curb and parks, but I don't pay it any attention. I would love to have a car to sleep in tonight, it would be cold, but at least it would be dry.

"Hey!" someone yells from behind me, the sound of feet moving quickly and getting closer makes me turn to look. "Hey, do I know you?" *No, but you sound like the voice I long to hear.*

I shake my head, attempting to move around the police officer. A light in my face blinds me for a minute before he drops the beam. "Yeah, aren't you a *friend* of Alister Bennet?"

At *his* name, my gaze snaps to the man's face standing in front of me, an exact replica of Alister. I stare at him, too emotionally broken to school my features. He moves the flashlight around, taking in the bags I'm carrying and the clothes sticking to my body from the water. "You okay? You need a lift somewhere?"

I open my mouth to tell him no, but nothing comes out, leaving me to just stare at him again. Too cold and tired to do anything else.

"I've got some towels in the squad car. Let's get you warmed up. Okay? Come sit in the car with me." He ushers me to the patrol car, removing the bags from my fingers. "Why don't you take your sweater off? I'll grab a blanket for you." He leaves me at the passenger side door and opens the trunk, digs around for a minute and comes back with a big brown blanket.

I can't get my sweater off without his help, my fingers not wanting to work. He notices me struggling and helps me pull my arms out of the sleeves, then lifts it over my head. Once it's off, he unfolds the blanket and wraps it around me, before helping me into the car where he blasts the heater. The warmth of the car burns my face, and the blanket makes me shiver harder than I was just a minute ago in the rain.

"Hey man, what's your name?"

It takes me a few tries to get the words past my trembling lips. "B- b- en."

"You know my brother, right? Alister Bennet?"

I nod, too exhausted to try to speak again.

"I'm Alex. Where are you walking to?"

I shrug my shoulders, the shaking of my body so intense I'm not sure he could see it. "Du- dun- no," I manage to get out.

"You don't know where you were going?"

My head shakes again.

"Um okay. Why are you wandering around in the rain for no reason?" He's starting to sound suspicious, and I can't blame him in the least, I sound insane. Or high.

"F- f- f- flood- ed." My teeth are chattering so hard I bite my tongue and it starts bleeding.

"Your place flooded?"

Not wanting blood to drip down my face, I keep my mouth closed and nod.

"You don't have anywhere to go? A friend or family member you can crash at?"

"N- no." The copper taste of blood is bitter in my mouth.

"How about Ali? I'm sure he would let you crash on his couch."

I shake my head but don't say anything, not sure what I can say. This is Alister's twin brother, nothing I say is going to end well for me.

Reaching for his phone, he does something and lifts it to his ear.

"Alex? Aren't you on duty?" Alister's voice comes across the line. Embarrassment has me leaning against the window and closing my eyes. My face is bright red from the cold, I'm sure, and my body is basically convulsing.

"Yeah, hey, I found your friend Ben, he appears to need a place to crash. He said his place flooded. I found him wandering around in the rain, completely soaked. I should probably take him to the hospital to be treated for hypothermia, but I think I caught him early enough, if we can get him warm, he'll be fine."

"Jesus Christ! Where did you find him? Can you bring him to my place?"

"Just a few streets over from you actually, we'll be there in a couple of minutes." He ends the call and starts driving, not asking if this is what I wanted, but since I don't have any other options… beggars can't be choosers.

"I don't know what's going on with you and my brother, but I know I've never seen anyone in his apartment before. He's mentioned you to me a few times, and he's never done that either, so you mean something to him."

I don't respond to him, just watch out the window. *Only a few streets down from Alister?* My subconscious wanted him, even if logic said I shouldn't.

Thirty

ALISTER

Alex's call definitely caught me off guard, he rarely calls me while on duty. He'll text if it's a really slow night, but most of the time he's patrolling. He found Ben just a few streets away from my apartment, drenched, and hypothermic, wandering around aimlessly. What the fuck is going on with him?

I pulled out a t-shirt and lounge pants with a drawstring for him to change into when he gets here, and some extra blankets to wrap around him. I don't know how bad he is, but pacing my living room floor isn't helping me stay calm. Yanking the front door open, I stalk to the elevator and hit the button to call the carriage. When the doors open, Alex is standing inside with a brown blanket wrapped around an exhausted and shivering Ben. Reaching for him, I wrap my arm around his shoulders and pull him to my side and into my place.

Inside, I lead Ben to the couch and have him sit so I can take off his shoes and socks. His feet are white, almost blue, and wrinkled from being wet for so long. From my place kneeling on the floor at his feet, I look up at his face. His lips are blue, jaw trembling, cheeks red, probably from Alex having the heater blasting in the car. Shivers are still racking his body, and I imagine they're better than they were. But his eyes, those deep pools, are full of defeat.

Alex clears his throat to get my attention. "He was carrying these, looks like mostly clothes. I'll put them by the washer and dryer for you guys to deal with later, do you need help getting him changed?"

"No, I got it, thanks. Thanks for calling me."

Alex disappears down the hallway, the opening and closing of sliding doors sounds, then he's back. "Let me know if you need anything. I'm on the night shift for a while, so I can swing stuff by on my way home if you need."

I nod but don't turn away from Ben. Alex leaves, the front door closing behind him, and we sit there for another moment. Shame and embarrassment flashes over his face.

"Can you stand? You need to get the wet clothes off in order to get warm. I've got some dry clothes you can put on."

He wobbles as he stands, my hand on his lower back helps keep him steady. His hands reach for the waist of his jeans, but his fingers fumble with the button.

"Can I help?" My voice is soft, trying to bring him comfort, and ease his embarrassment. This isn't exactly the way I wanted to get him out of his pants for the first time.

His shoulders sag even farther, and his hands drop, his forehead leaning into my chest. Making quick work of the button and zipper, I work his jeans and the elastic of his underwear down his hips and over his ass, far enough for him to sit. Getting wet denim off is always a pain in the ass, but I work as quickly as I can to free him from the fabric. Taking the blanket from his shoulders, I lift the t-shirt over his head and drop it on the floor with the rest of the wet clothes.

I grab one of my extra blankets and wrap it around him, and the soft plush fabric is dry and soothing against his irritated skin. "Do you want to put clothes on or are you okay naked? We should lay down together. My body heat will help get you warmed up."

When he doesn't answer, I wrap my arm around his shoulders, help him stand, and steer him toward my bedroom. The blankets on my bed are pulled down, making it easy to slide him in. I strip my clothes off and slip in the other side, pulling him against my chest. His skin is freezing, almost painful to have against mine, but I force myself to stay wrapped around him. His body needs to warm up, or I'll have no choice but to take him to the hospital.

His face nuzzles into my neck, brushing the mark he left this morning, and with one arm around my back with our legs intertwined, he falls asleep. He's not just asleep but passed out, completely dead to the world, exhaustion forcing his body to shut down. I wrap my arms around him tighter and hold him, so fucking glad to have him with me, even if the circumstances are terrible.

In a few hours, my skin is slick with sweat. Ben is still wrapped around me, but he's no longer shivering. With the way the night unfolded, I didn't close my curtains before laying down. A small break in the clouds lets enough of the moonlight in for me to see the color is back in his face, and that he's dreaming peacefully. Careful not to wake him, I move the heavy blanket off us, leaving us covered in only a flannel sheet.

I'm finding myself at war with what I want at this moment. I want to kiss him awake, show him without words how much he means to me, let my body worship his, the way he deserves. But I also want to just hold him, be the safe place he needs right now. He shouldn't have to worry about being taken advantage of while he sleeps, so I'll stay here and watch over him, no matter what my dick says.

Ben has been here for a few days, mostly just sleeping and eating. He spiked a fever the morning after he got here, I'm not sure if it was from the hypothermia, but his stomach has been okay, so I've been trying to force ibuprofen and Tylenol into him along with soup, bread, and water. I wasn't able to get into his student email, so I had to call his professors, try to disguise my voice and leave messages to excuse the absences. I was too worried to leave him alone all day, so I had to excuse myself from classes as well. Hopefully canceling one class won't set anyone too far behind.

The sun is shining directly in my face, blinding me before I open my eyes. It takes me a minute to realize Ben is behind me, pressed against my back, his cock nestled in my ass cheeks. It's been a long time since I bottomed, but I am more than willing. In his sleep, he moves against me, his body seeking pleasure.

Feeling him rubbing against me, skin to skin is almost more than I can take. Blood thrums through my veins, hardening every muscle in my body, my fists ball into the sheets. Finding his rhythm, I push back into his thrusts, wanting to feel him move inside of me. It's not long before he tenses and freezes, waking up and realizing what he's feeling isn't just a dream. His hands on my hips flex and release as he tries to regain control over himself.

Ben releases my hips and drops onto his back, throwing an arm over his eyes. Turning toward him, my thigh sliding in between his, I kiss my way up his chest. This may have started while he was asleep, but I'll be damned if he's ashamed now that he's awake. Spreading his thighs with my knees, my tongue and lips explore his chest, groaning when his hips move against mine. My lips capture his, our tongues twisting and sliding together in a dance all our own. Ben's thighs cradle my hips perfectly, our bodies connected from hip to lips, still soft from sleep.

My lips capture his whimpers, sparking the fire in my blood to burn hotter, my need for him climbing. Moving together, our cocks are trapped between us as we grind against each other. Pulling my mouth from his, my forehead drops to his shoulder. "If you tell me to stop, I will." It will kill me, but I'll walk away from him if he's not ready.

"No, please," he breathes against my ear, and the whimper in his voice almost does me in. Forcing my eyes to meet his, I need to make sure he's thinking this through. I don't want him to regret this later once the lust has cleared.

"Ben, look at me." It takes a minute, but the deep obsidian of his eyes meets mine. "Do you want this? Do you want me to fuck you?"

Lust glazes over his features, and for a split second he freezes, before jumping into action. Both hands grip my ass and press me into his stomach, the heels of his feet digging into me. "Fuck me."

Reaching for the bedside table, I rip the drawer open and blindly search for lube, knocking stuff over in my impatient search. Finally finding it, I sit back on my knees and pop the top of lube open. Breathing hard, Ben's eyes lock on mine as a lube covered finger finds the tight muscle of his ass.

"Relax, babe. I'm going to make you feel good." The tension in his body lessons, my finger pressing inside to just the first knuckle. Holding my finger still, I let him get used to the sensation and pressure. Ben's back arches off the bed with the slightest movement from my finger, the taut ring squeezing me so tight. It's not long before a second finger is added, pumping slowly into his ass.

"Please, I want to feel you." His whine makes my dick ache, and a pearl of precum leaks from my tip.

"Do you want me to wear a condom? I won't be offended if you do." I don't want to, I want to feel him skin-to-skin, but I'll wear it if he's more comfortable.

"No, just you." Flipping open the lube once again, I make sure my length is slick and lean over him, lining my cock up with his hole. My dick is thicker than my fingers, and he tenses against the intrusion. "Take a deep breath for me and relax. Do you trust me?"

His eyes catch mine, and he nods, biting on his lip in nervousness. With some force, my tip slips in before he clenches around me, a deep groan rumbling my chest. Dropping to my elbows, I crash my lips to his, slowly pushing the rest of the way inside of him. Ben wraps his arms around my neck, ravaging my mouth with nips, licks, and sucks, all the while I'm pumping slowly in and out of his ass. Sliding my forearms under his back, I grip his shoulders, pressing our bodies together, slick with sweat as I take his ass for the first time.

The grip on his shoulders changes the angle, and from the change in Ben's moans, I'm sure my dick is stroking his prostate, turning the already pleasurable act much more intense. "Fuck," he whimpers in my ear. "Alister, please." My pace increases, pumping faster and harder into his tight, hot ass. My balls draw up, and a tingle starts at my lower back, I'm ready to cum deep inside him.

His back bows seconds before hot spurts of cum coat my stomach as my orgasm rocks me hard, making me thrust roughly and filling him with me. We lay there breathing hard, trembling from the physical and emotional force of our orgasms.

Thirty-One

BEN

THE HOT WATER SCALDS my skin, but I take a few minutes to enjoy it and remember the feel of Alister on my skin. The memory of him inside of me sends a shiver over me and goosebumps cover my skin. We laid on the bed, wrapped around each other for a few minutes. I've never experienced anything like this before, the physical release was mind-blowing, but the emotional connection, the care he took to make sure I was okay and comfortable, was more than anyone has ever given me.

Shaking the thoughts away, I don't remember the last hot shower I had—it's been years. Being here is a mind fuck, I don't understand why he would let me in. A few days ago, I came on his stomach and told him I didn't want to see him anymore. The hurt in his eyes almost made me take it back, to beg him to forgive me. The day kept getting worse, ending with me wandering the streets, drenched, freezing, and homeless.

But, I had sex with Alister Bennet.

A smile breaks out on my face that I can't stop, not that I want to. I know I should keep him at arm's length, I'll get my heart broken when he realizes he can do better than me, but I'm not strong enough. I'm not strong enough to walk away again, I tried, and ended up in his bed. At what point do I get what I want? What I deserve?

Scrubbing cum off my body with Alister's body wash, No. 63 scents the steam. I like smelling him on my skin, and I feel more confident, protected. The steam has filled the small room and guilt sets in for using so much of the hot water. Rinsing the suds off, I shut the water off and grab my towel. The towel is so much softer than I'm used to, fluffier or something. Wrapping it around my hips, I go back into Alister's bedroom and find the bed has been made and clothes have been set out for me, his clothes. He's taking care of me. No one has ever done that for me before. I've had to beg, take beatings, for everything I've ever had.

The white V-neck t-shirt is huge on me, but it's comfortable, and the grey lounge pants have a drawstring to keep them up. Otherwise, they would be at my ankles. Wearing his clothes reinstates how skinny I am, how underweight I am.

Shaking my head to clear it, I leave the bedroom in search of Alister. I want to give this a chance. I want to know what it's like to be able to touch someone, simply because I want to. To know what it's like to know I don't have to be alone, that I can share my day with him, relax with him.

Hearing noise from the kitchen, I peek around the corner to see Alister at the stove. He's so comfortable here, in his element, confident in his movements. I stand off to the side where he's not likely to see me and watch him for a few minutes, enjoying the way his muscles move under his shirt. My dick is hardening again, the soft fabric of the lounge pants doing nothing to hide it.

Entering the room, I wrap my arms around his waist and lay my cheek against his back. For the first time in my life, I'm touching someone because I want to. I took the first step, I touched him first. The steady thump of Alister's heart beats in my ear. A warm hand covers mine on his stomach.

"Hey, breakfast is almost done. How are you feeling? What would you like to drink?" This moment is so normal, and something I've never had.

"I feel good, thanks. I think I'll have coffee."

Turning in my arms, he faces with me with a raised eyebrow. "Oh yeah? This morning is full of firsts for you."

Up on my toes, I press my lips to his, a gentle, easy kiss. A thank you. His arms are loose around me, content at the moment. Dropping back down, I smile at him, a real smile I can feel to my soul. "That's another first."

Cocking his head, he looks at me. "What is? We've kissed before."

"But I haven't been the one to start it. I touched you first. I've never done that with anyone else before." I'm slightly embarrassed by my revelation, but he knows I'm not experienced. "Though, technically, I've had sex before. It just wasn't with a man."

"Really?" He turns back to the stove and plates our breakfast. "I would like to hear the story if you don't mind sharing it." Handing me the plates, I take them to the table while he makes me a cup of coffee. Seating us across the table from each other, he brings in the steaming mugs, cream, and sugar. I haven't had coffee often, but I know I hate it black, so I add cream and sugar to my cup before tasting it.

My eyes close as my hands wrap around the hot cup, the sweet, creamy drink warming me from the inside as it slides down my throat.

"Damn that was sexy." Alister's voice startles me. "I didn't mean to make you jump." He chuckles.

My cheeks flush. "It's really good."

"I'm glad you're enjoying it." He takes a bite of his eggs and watches me while he chews.

"How long have I been here?"

"Well, it's Thursday, so about two and a half days."

I'm stunned. *Two days?* "Why did you let me stay? Why did you have Alex bring me here in the first place?"

"Well, I told Alex to bring you here because you were in trouble and I wanted to help. And you've been sick. I wasn't going to leave you unconscious somewhere."

I don't have a response, because I can't wrap my head around him helping me in the first place. People aren't nice to me without a reason, except Kristen.

"So, care to tell me about the girl?" Alister's voice brings me back to the here and now.

Thinking of Kristen makes me smile and feel guilty at the same time, I shouldn't have talked to her like I did the other day. I need to call her. "Her name is Kristen, and she's been my best friend since I was about nine."

"That's a long time. Does she live locally?"

"Not anymore, she got accepted as a transfer student to Cal Poly about a year ago."

"Cal Poly? That's damn impressive. How did you meet her?"

"I was the new kid at school, and for some reason, she took pity on me. I've always been skinny, and she is the image of perfection. Blonde with blue eyes, looks sweet and innocent, but once she opens her mouth you know she's not. She never went through that awkward stage either, she always looked good. Her family is loaded, you can see it from a mile away, but she decided I was her best friend my first day."

"Sounds like a good friend to have."

"She was, is. I was always bullied until Kristen threatened to get everyone's parents fired from their jobs. Her father has a lot of power so everyone believed she could do it. When we were freshmen, we dated. I was pretty sure I wasn't into girls, but my foster parent was crazy, and if he thought I was gay, it would have been bad." I don't want Alister to know how bad it was growing up, and I don't want him to pity me. "So, being the awesome girl she is, she agreed to date me all through high school. We would purposefully get caught making out, trying to make it believable. Well, at one point, we decided to give sex a shot. We were both virgins, and she said she would rather lose it to me, her best friend, than to some jackass."

I'm pushing my food around my plate, nervous at his reaction. I don't want to look at him, but I want to know his reaction at the same time.

"Ben." Taking a deep breath, I look at him and see him smirking at me. "We all go through it. I had a girlfriend in high school."

It's nice to talk to someone who went through the uncertainty, the fear of being judged.

"I hope I get to meet Kristen someday."

I can't help but laugh, if only he knew. "I'm pretty sure she knows more about you, than you do."

"Huh? What does that mean?"

"Before she transferred, she was given an assignment in one of her journalism classes to research a professor on campus. They were not allowed to talk to the professor they were doing a mock-up article about, but had to find out as much information as they could by asking associates, Google, former students, stuff like that. She picked you."

"Me? Why on earth would she pick me? I'm not that interesting."

"Because you're the hottest teacher we have, you're never seen with anyone in a dating situation, and you don't wear a ring. Girls are obsessed with you."

He chuckles and sits back in his chair, taking a drink of his coffee. "Just girls? Have you seen my ass? It's pretty awesome."

A smile lifts my lips, laughing at his ridiculous question. "I'm pretty sure I saw it, once."

He drains his cup and stands to take his dishes to the kitchen, stopping, he gives me a pointed look. "Eat."

I scoop up a big bite of eggs and shove it in my mouth, making a big show of eating. The smile he flashes me has my heartbeat increasing, because he's the most attractive man I've ever seen.

"I have to get ready for school. Do you want to walk with me?"

"I don't have any clothes to wear. Mine are all wet."

He nods, thinking. "Shit, I'm sorry. I forgot all about them. Do you have morning classes? We can toss your clothes in the washer and dryer, but you won't make it to campus until the afternoon."

"You can get dressed and go. I'll figure it out." My eyes drop back to my plate. I don't want him to think I need him to solve my problems for me.

The sound of the plate on the table has my head lifting in confusion. Alister grasps my cheeks in his hands and kisses me hard, ravaging my lips. His teeth nip at my bottom lip until I open for him and groan when his tongue dances with mine. I melt under his intensity. Pulling back, he waits to speak until my eyes meet his. "Don't brush me off. I want to help. I want to know you're taken care of, that you're okay, and the only way I can know for sure is to take care of you myself."

"Why? Why do you care so much?" My insecurities are choking me. I know I'm ruining this moment, but I can't stop it.

"I'm not sure why it's so important to me, but it is. You're in my head all the time. 'What are you doing? Have you eaten? Are you okay?' Those thoughts are constantly running through my brain." His thumb caresses my cheek softly. "You're important to me, Ben." He lays a kiss on my forehead before walking into his bedroom to take a shower.

I locate the washer and dryer and dig through the pitiful number of things I own, dropping the wet clothes into the drum. It's hard not to think of my life as pathetic when everything I own fits into a few bags. *How long will it take for Alister to kick me out? How long before he's bored with my inexperience and tired of my insecurities?*

"What are you thinking so hard about?" Cinnamon and nutmeg fills the air in the hallway as he exits his room, clean and dressed for class. He stops beside me, his hand on my lower back.

"How long it'll take for you to get bored with me." I regret the words the second they leave my mouth. Shame heats my cheeks and my head drops to hang from my shoulders.

Turning me to face him, I resign myself to the conversation he's going to want. "Why would I get bored with you?"

A humorless laugh is forced from me. "Why wouldn't you? I'm inexperienced, homeless, and basically a walking insecurity. Why would you want to be around the walking definition of depression? I suck the life out of everyone around me, and my only friend moved to a different state to get away from me!" I slam the lid of the washer down and storm down the hallway, but don't have anywhere to go from there. Standing in the living room with my hands on my hips, I'm angry and frustrated.

I don't know how to do this, how to be normal. I don't know how to interact with people or be in a relationship. The only thing I'm good at is being a whipping boy, a punching bag.

Alister's footsteps come down the hallway and stop behind me, but he doesn't touch me this time, for some reason, and that hurts. "I don't know what you've been through, but it doesn't define who you are. I know your life is a mess, your apartment flooded, you're trying to graduate, you're dealing with the emotions that come with your first gay experiences, but I'm a patient man. Lean on me, talk to me, just *be* with me, and the rest will fall into place.

"Don't worry about trying to find a new apartment. You can stay here. If you want your own space, I can make up the spare room for you, but I like having you in my bed." He takes a deep breath and lets it out, the exhale brushing my neck. "I'm heading to campus. I can wait to leave campus until you're done with classes, if you want. All you have to do is tell me what you want, what you need. I'll happily give you anything I can."

His body presses against me, and his arms wrap around my waist. One hand flattens over my heart, and his lips brush the base of my neck, then he's walking toward the door. "There's a key on the kitchen counter and my cell phone number." He doesn't wait for a response, just shuts the door, leaving me to deal with the fact that I'm an asshole.

Thirty-Two

ALISTER

This morning didn't go as I had expected, both in good and bad ways. Sex with Ben was so much *more* than it's ever been with anyone else, so much better, every touch more pleasurable.

The more I learn about him, the more I want to know. I know growing up was hard, he wouldn't have the trust and confidence issues he has if his childhood was good, but just how bad was it? It will probably break me to hear his story, to know the struggles and pain he's endured, but I know it has made him the person he is today.

A notification on my phone grabs my attention, bringing me back to the present. Grabbing the device, I notice the time and hurry to get to class. Power walking to the classroom, I open the message from an unknown number.

Unknown: I'm sorry I lost it this morning. Thank you for everything you've done for me.

Smiling at the message, I don't have time to respond, but I'm glad he reached out. Starting today's lesson, I'm feeling lighter than I have in days, hopeful for what the future will bring.

After back-to-back classes all morning, I finally get back to my office and have an hour before office hours start. I turn on the Keurig and take a seat behind my desk, the overhead light is off to discourage people from bothering me. I've been a little busy in my off hours lately, a little distracted, so I've fallen behind.

Grabbing a mug off the hook on the wall, I get coffee flowing when a soft knock on the door pulls my attention. I contemplate ignoring it, but whoever is on the other side opens the door. Messy black hair and obsidian eyes peek through the opening and catch me watching. Ben freezes for a second then smiles, coming inside and closing the door behind him.

"Hey, I wasn't expecting to see you this early." Pulling him into a hug, I drop a quick kiss on his lips.

"Thursday's are all morning classes, except my damn Calculus class. That professor is a real ball buster." My smile is so big it's starting to hurt my cheeks, but my heart is so fucking happy. He's cracking jokes, at my expense no less, and it hurts my heart in the best possible way.

"He sounds like a real dick."

Ben chuckles, a smile taking over his lips and making his eyes sparkle. He shrugs a shoulder. "It's actually a pretty nice dick."

I back him up to the filing cabinet, trapping him. "Mr. Wallace, are you flirting with me?"

"I believe I am, Mr. Bennet, what are you going to do about it?" He leans forward and nips at my lips, before sealing his against mine. I love that he's getting some confidence, my dick is happy about it as well, throbbing against the zipper of my pants. The kiss is ending when a thought occurs to me.

"I think you've only used my first name once this morning."

A blush reddens his cheeks, and he knows I've caught him talking about me. "Well…"

"Who were you talking to about me?" I can't stop the smug satisfaction.

"Kristen."

"I would love to meet her next time she's in town." I kiss his forehead and take a seat behind my desk, grabbing my coffee from the Keurig. "Does she visit often? Have family here?"

"She hasn't visited since she transferred a year ago, but she does have family here, I'm pretty sure they're the reason she hasn't come back though. She has a difficult relationship with her parents." Ben drops down on the chair and relaxes. It's one of the few times I've seen him this way.

"That's too bad. Hey, speaking of parents, I have weekly dinners with mine on Thursdays, would you like to go?"

Just like that, he's stiff as a board and as tense as a bowstring. "You want me to meet your parents?"

"Yeah, I do. Maybe next week or come to Thanksgiving in a few weeks? They'll like you, I promise."

"I don't know…"

"Just think about it, okay? If you don't want to go, you don't have to, but I'll be there to run interference." He's looking at his hands, obviously uncomfortable, and I hate that I'm the reason.

Focusing on inputting grades, I barely see his nod as he grabs his backpack and gets to work on homework.

"When am I ever going to need to know how to find the differential of x when the limit goes to infinity? Never!" Ben's outburst startles me, making me jump when he slams the book closed.

"Would you like some help?" I try to keep the smile from lifting my lips, but I fail miserably.

"No. What I want is not to have to take this stupid class. What I want is for you to tell me I can suck your dick and you'll pass me." He turns to me, blazing eyes locking on my surprised ones.

"Well, sucking my dick isn't going to *hurt* your grade." Ben stands and stalks toward me, spins my chair to face him, and drops to his knees, never diverting his eyes from mine. Ben's hands slide up my thighs, my cock hard and aching behind the zipper. My belt, button, and zipper open easily under his nimble fingers. A groan escapes me when his hand wraps around me, pulling me free from the confines of my jeans. Sliding my ass down the seat a bit, I lean back in the chair to give him more room.

Coughing in the hallway has us freezing, his mouth an inch from my tip. Ben shifts, so most of his body is under my desk and drops my chair to give him room before pulling the chair in. Should someone come through the door, they will be none the wiser that a fantasy is playing out in the room.

Not being able to see him heightens the sensations, his hot breath against my skin, the squeeze of his hand while he pumps me, then the surprise of a hot wet mouth surrounding my tip. My head drops back against the chair, my hips flex, wanting farther into the paradise that is Ben's mouth. He's exploring my length, licking, kissing, and sucking on the hardened flesh while he gets familiar with it. Having never done this before, he's doing a damn fine job of driving me insane.

The office door opens with a knock, a young co-ed enters with a blush on her cheeks and a shy smile. *Fuck.* Movement under the desk stops, enabling me to get a deep breath. "Hello, how can I help you?" My voice squeaks and cracks like a pre-teen whose voice is just starting to change. Ben's hand slides down my length in time with his mouth and my toes curl in my shoes.

She gives me a strange look and cocks her head to the side. Narrowing her eyes, she takes a look around, taking notice of Ben's stuff on the table. Gone is the blushing, shy young girl, and in her place is a calculating young woman, putting together pieces of a puzzle. "Where is he?" Her voice is strong, direct.

Once again Ben freezes. "Wh- who?" I manage to force out.

"Benjamin Wallace."

She has my attention now. I take a second to look her over, blonde hair in two braids, blue eyes, petite but curvy. Light blue jeans that look custom made for her and a slim fitting, blue Fraggle Rock t-shirt under an off-white cardigan finishes off her look. She reminds me of the girls Alex goes for. *How does she know Ben and what does she want?*

Before I have a chance to ask, I'm being pushed back into the wall, and Ben's head pops up from under the desk. Scrambling to get myself put away while he's blocking me, it's completely clear what was going on since my dick is still out. "Kristen!"

Ben rushes to her and throws his arms around her in a tight hug. Once I've gotten myself put back together, I stand and watch the two childhood friends. He's so relaxed with her, evident by the big smile on his face. He looks so much younger without the worry and fears weighing on him.

"Hey," she laughs, hugging him just as tightly. "Surprise!"

"What are you doing here?"

"Well, when my best friend's apartment floods, we get into a fight, then he stops talking to me, something has to be done."

A deep sigh leaves him with drooping shoulders and his head hangs low. "I'm sorry. I was an asshole. I wanted to call you, but things have been a little crazy."

"Yeah, I got that when I walked in and you were giving your teacher a blowie under his desk. Times sure have changed." She laughs again, making the situation feel lighter. Stepping around Ben she holds her hand out to me to shake. "Kristen Collins, nice to meet you, Mr. Bennet."

"Alister, please. It's nice to meet you too Kristen."

Ben looks between us, happy but hesitant at the same time. "Kris, it's been three days. Why are you really here?"

She shrugs one shoulder. "Finding you was the most important reason, but I was called home by my parents. My uncle died, and I have to *pay my respects,* though I would rather spit on his grave." She rolls her eyes.

"I'm so sorry for your family's loss, Kristen," I offer, but she brushes it away.

"He was a terrible person, good riddance." She wraps her arm around Ben's waist and leans into him.

"Ben, since you're done with classes for the day, why don't you guys head back to the apartment? Spend some time together and catch up?" I want him to feel like my place is somewhere he can call home. This thing between us is moving fast, but it feels right to have him there.

Kristen raises an eyebrow and looks up at Ben. "The apartment? Did you move in with your boyfriend and not tell me?"

That's the first time the term "boyfriend" has been used, and I'm not sure how Ben is going to react to it. The butterflies in my stomach and the smile on my face should tell him I like the label. Ben's eyes widen, his cheeks flush, and he stammers, "Oh, well…um…shit."

"He's staying with me for now, since his apartment is uninhabitable."

"Hmmm," is Kristen's response. "I'm hungry, get your stuff and feed me."

"The she-beast is hungry, that doesn't bode well for me." Turning to the table, he starts picking up his books and shoving them into his backpack. I join him at the chair to help and to be closer to him. "Have fun with your friend, I'll see you later."

He turns to me with a smile. "Thank you."

"You're welcome." I give him a chaste kiss and whisper in his ear, "we can finish the blow job later too."

Ben chuckles, grabs his bag and swings it over his shoulder as he moves to the door with his best friend. "See you at home," I call to him.

With the biggest smile I've ever seen on him, he says, "See you at home." My heart flutters at his words, contentment and happiness settling in my chest.

Thirty-Three

BEN

ARM IN ARM WITH Kristen, I finally feel like my life is going right. For once. I didn't realize just how empty my life was without her here to force me to live. I've been surviving for so long I don't really know how to live, I never really did. My whole life has been just surviving the latest catastrophe, the last beating, or trying to avoid the next one.

"Earth to Ben!" Her hand waves in my face.

"Sorry, I got lost in my head. What were you saying?"

"I was saying he's good for you. You look happy."

My eyes roll back into my head far enough for me to see my brain. "I've been around him for a few days. It's way too early for that."

"When someone is right, you just know. You don't have to be around them very long." Her voice is wistful, not something I'm used to.

"What's up with you?"

"What? Everyone wants to find love."

I scoff at her. "What happened to 'I don't need a man'?" My imitation of her is so bad she laughs.

"I don't *need* a man, but I would like to fall in love. Have dick at the ready every night." I laugh, there's the Kris I know.

I'm heading toward the bus stop out of habit when she pulls me toward the parking lot. "I have a car. You know my father wouldn't let me use public transportation, even if my life depended on it."

We get settled in the car, the heater blasting warm air, and make our way to Alister's apartment. The key he gave me is safely tucked inside my wallet since I no longer have a key ring. I can't get over the fact that I'm staying here. That I'm in the early stages of a relationship with an amazing man who is so fucking sexy it should be illegal.

"This is a nice place," Kristen says as we enter the apartment.

"I know. I really like it here."

"Look at you! All smiles. I fucking love it."

Shaking my head at her, I drop my backpack in the chair and head to the fridge for some water bottles. Back in the living room, I plop down on the couch next to Kris and hand her a bottle of water. Leaning back against the pillows, she looks at me with a smile that means trouble.

"So, have you had sex with him yet?" Her eyebrows wag.

"As a matter-of-fact, yes."

She jolts upright and spins around to stare at me. "Seriously? Tell me everything!"

Her expression is priceless, shocked and excited all rolled into one. "Just this morning actually."

"What?" Her arms fly around, which tells me she's really shocked. "How did you end up here anyway?"

"His brother, Alex, saw me walking down the street with some bags and brought me here." I don't need to tell her I was soaking wet and in the first stage of hypothermia.

"What are the odds? He was just driving around?"

"He's a police officer and was driving his route or whatever it's called."

"That's crazy. And he just brought you here? What if you and Alister were on the outs?"

"He called Alister once I was in the car, and he told Alex to bring me here. It was kind of surreal. But since I had had a rough day, he laid down with me in his bed, and we fell asleep." Skipping all the bad parts, and the fact I was unconscious for two days, makes my day sound pretty normal…

"And? How did that end in sex?"

Sarcasm drips from my words. "Well, when two grown-ups are attracted to each other, they show it in a physical manner." Kristen grabs a pillow and throws it at me, hitting me in the chest. "We woke up with hard-ons, you know how it goes."

"I don't, in fact, know what it's like to wake up with a hard-on. I'm not sure how you missed that little fact when we had sex." She rolls her eyes at me and crosses her arms under her chest.

"Hey, you could have had a sex change since then. It's not like I see you naked all the time."

She stands up and faces me, her hands wave in front of hips. "Do you think there is room in these jeans for a dick?"

I make a show of looking, staring at her and contemplating. "Well, I guess if it was really small."

With a yell, she tackles me. Pinching and tickling me until I beg for mercy.

"Well, what do we have here?" An amused voice has us jumping and spinning toward the entryway. "Hey Ben, your circumstances look better than the last time I saw you. You doing alright?" Alex asks, standing in the living room, in uniform. His hair is shorter than Alister's and he doesn't have a beard, but he's built exactly the same. In the short sleeves of his uniform, the sleeves of tattoos on his arms are on display too.

"Yeah, thanks."

"Do you normally barge into your brother's apartment when he's not home?" Kristen asks, cocking her head.

Alex looks her over, head to foot. Obviously appreciating the way she looks. "Well, since I have a key, yeah I do. You seem to know who I am, but who are you, beautiful?"

"Uck. My name is Kristen. Please don't give me nicknames."

"Sure, blondie, whatever you say. My name is Alex, by the way." He holds his hand out for her to shake, but Kristen just looks down her nose at it.

She rolls her eyes, squares her shoulders, and crosses her arms under her chest again. Getting ready for a verbal sparring match I'm almost certain Alex will lose.

"*Alister's brother* is fine with me. When you start using my name, I'll consider using yours."

Alex steps closer, getting into Kristen's personal space, but she refuses to back down. "Oh, pretty young thing, I can't wait to learn more about you. You're a firecracker. I'd be all too happy to show around."

"You are so full of yourself, I don't know how you don't choke on it. You think because your arms are the same size as your head, women will just fall to their knees and worship you? Sorry, I'm not that kind of girl."

"Sorry, I didn't catch most of that. I got distracted by the image of you choking while on your knees at my feet." The smile that takes over his face is full of sexual promises, he's not looking at me, but I can feel the heat from his gaze.

"My oh my, aren't you charming? You have a real way with words, Officer Bennet. I think my panties just disintegrated." Her mocking tone makes me snort, miss high and mighty comes out to play every once in a while.

Alex throw his head back and laughs, enjoying the shit out of himself. "I think I love you," he says with a wink as he walks off down the hall.

Spinning on me, Kristen is fired up. "Can you believe that guy? What an asshole!"

"He's like that all the time," is the only thing I can think to say.

The toilet flushes, followed by the sound of water running, before a door opens, and Alex's footsteps are heard coming back toward us. "Ben, glad to see you've got your color back. Hope to see you at Thanksgiving dinner." He nods to me before turning to Kristen. "Hope to see you again real soon too, sweet cheeks." He winks again then disappears, and the front door closes.

"I need a damn drink. What a Neanderthal." She stomps off toward the kitchen, leaving me snickering on the couch. It's not very often someone can get under Kristen's skin like this. "What the hell?" she yells from the kitchen. "Ben! There is no food in here! Only things to make food!"

Coming back to the living room, she grabs her phone and flips a few things. "I'm ordering pizza. What's the address?"

I rattle it off and try to think of the last time I had pizza. It was probably with her…

"Thirty minutes until delivery, I might be able to survive that long."

I shake my head at her, for such a small person, she eats a ton of food. Her world revolves around eating, but it's nice to know I won't starve when she's around. Small comforts.

Thirty-Four

ALISTER

When I get home a few hours later, Kristen and Ben are lying out on the couch watching a movie, an empty pizza box is on the coffee table with an empty lava cake box inside of it. It looks like a college dorm room. Shoes were kicked off in front of the couch, blankets are haphazard across them, and multiple water bottles litter the floor and table.

Smiling at the two of them, I stand and watch them for a minute. It makes me happy to see Ben doing something so typical of his age. Most of the time it's like he doesn't realize he's twenty-three and should be out partying, getting drunk with friends, and falling asleep hugging a toilet.

"Looks like you guys are enjoying yourselves." Ben's head jerks, his eyes holding fear and uncertainty. Putting my bag down with his backpack on the chair, I come around to where he's sitting, lean down, and kiss him.

nly meaning for it to be a brushing of lips, but when his hand holds onto the back of my neck, I give in and kiss him the way I want to. The logical part of my brain says it's rude to kiss him like this in front of his friend, but the man kissing his lover part of my brain says, "do it anyway."

I force myself to back off, to end the kiss with a soft brush of lips, Ben's whimper of disappointment going straight to my groin.

"Fuck that was hot." Kristen's comment makes me chuckle.

"Sorry about that," I say, shrugging a shoulder.

"I'm not," Ben pipes up, all of us smiling at the outburst.

"Ben, come with me for a second?" Reaching for his hand, he's quick to intertwine our fingers and follow along behind me into the bedroom.

Once the door is closed behind us, he drops my hand and starts picking at his nails. "I'm sorry, I lost track of time. I'll get the living room cleaned up the way you like it." The worry in his voice cuts through the haze of lust from just a moment ago.

"Hey," I say, pulling him closer to me with my hands on his hips. "It's fine. You're having a good time with your best friend who you haven't seen in a while. I'm not mad. It makes me happy to see you comfortable and enjoying yourself." My lips brush against his, physically showing him I'm not upset. "I'll help you get everything cleaned up later."

Ben smiles up at me and wraps his arms around my neck. "Are you just trying to sweet talk me, so I'll suck your dick again?"

I throw my head back and laugh, that was definitely not what I was expecting. I love that he's joking and flirting with me. "Maybe."

Rescue Me

He smiles back at me, lifting onto his toes to kiss me again, slow and sensual this time. Sliding lips and dancing tongues, soft sighs. "If you want to, you can come watch the movie with us."

"I would love to, let me get changed and I'll be right there."

Turning to head back to the living room, I stop him with a hand on his shoulder. "I liked when she called me your boyfriend."

"Yeah?"

"Yeah, I did."

"I liked it too," he admits.

"Good." I smile at him and kiss him again. "That's good, because I want everyone to know you're mine."

"I want everyone to know too." His voice is quiet, cheeks turning pink. He buries his face in my chest, hugging me hard. "I'll go to Thanksgiving dinner at your parents' house."

I wrap my arms around him, knowing how hard it is for him, grateful for his trust in me to protect him.

Kristen had to meet up with her family, though she wasn't very enthused about it, but promised to stop by again before she flies back to California. The door closes behind her and Ben gets a lost puppy look on his face. I have a feeling she made a lot of the decisions for him, took control of situations so he wouldn't have to stand up for himself, so he feels lost without her.

Pulling him into my chest with my arm around his shoulders, I lead him to the bedroom so I can get changed. His clothes are folded and stacked on the bed. I like his stuff being in here.

"Did you have a good time with Kristen?" I ask, unbuttoning my shirt and smirking when Ben's eyes follow the movement.

"Uh, yeah." He's watching me as I change, the black of his eyes becoming endless as lust covers his gaze.

"I'll clear out some drawer space for your clothes tonight, feel free to hang up whatever you need to." Walking toward Ben, he backs into the dresser, which is exactly where I'm heading. Laying my hands on either side of him, I cage him against it and lean into his space. "I would much rather have you for dinner, but dessert will just have to do."

His breath catches, and his hands rub up my abdomen, chest, and wrap around my neck. Pressing my body against his, I growl and bite at his plump lower lip before sucking it into my mouth. My cock is hard, the zipper of my pants indenting the flesh while I thrust against the man wrapped around me. My balls are heavy and ache from being denied release earlier. It's not long before I'm desperate, the need to cum shutting down logic. Moving my hands from the dresser to my pants, I free my erection and fist myself to relieve some pressure.

One of Ben's hands slides down to cup my balls gently, and I groan into his mouth. I take a step back, my blood on fire as I tell Ben to kneel, my tone leaving no room for argument. Immediately, he's on his knees, looking up at me with anticipation. Licking his lips, his eyes drop to my cock, which is level with his mouth. "Open."

The need to be in his mouth, pushing the limits of his gag reflex, has my language cut to one-word commands. Ben's mouth opens, and he leans forward, enveloping the purple head with wet heat. My hand drops away as his takes over, working in tandem with his mouth to create a rotating, hot suction.

My eyelids want to close, but I refuse to give in, I need to watch every second of Ben pleasuring me. His eyes are on mine, molten, driven to insanity by the power he has over me. My balls draw up tight, the tingle at my spine intensifies, and my hand reaches for his hair. "I'm gonna cum." Those three words are the only warning he gets, approximately half a second before hot jets shoot down his throat. The power of my orgasm has me leaning a hand against the dresser, knees wobbling when Ben's strokes become lazy and his other hand cups my balls.

My eyes finally win over and close, as I tremble and try to keep my knees from giving out. "Fuck."

"That was the hottest thing I've ever seen, ever been a part of." Awe softens his voice and makes me chuckle.

"I'm happy to be your plaything again, anytime. That was amazing. Thank you."

Ben stands, puts my half hard dick back into my pants, then zips and buttons me. I'm still leaning against the dresser, afraid my legs won't hold my weight. He kisses my breastbone, licks one nipple and bites the other, sucks his way up my neck, before ravaging my mouth. Blood once again heads to my groin, and heat fires my veins. Standing up straight, I tangle both hands in his hair, pulling him up against me. "You're playing a dangerous game. I haven't missed family dinner in years, but I will, just to fuck you into oblivion."

He chuckles, licking his lower lip. "Are you sure you can get it up again? It's pretty quick for a man your age."

My eyes widen in shock. "Did you just crack an age joke? Are you saying I can't keep up with your twenty-year-old sex drive? It will be my pleasure to prove you wrong." My voice is rough like I've smoked a pack a day all my life.

Goosebumps erupt over Ben's skin, and a shaky breath leaves him, telling me just how much he likes it when I get a little alpha. Never in my life have I wanted to dominate or control anyone, but I'm finding this a huge turn on right now. I want to prove myself to him. I want to show him he can trust me, that I won't ever hurt him. I'm so grateful he's chosen to explore his sexuality with me, and I'm beyond honored.

"When do you need to leave?" Ben's voice brings my attention back to the present. Glancing at the clock, I mutter under my breath and grab a t-shirt from the drawer.

Pulling it over my head, I kiss him again, shove my arms through the holes, and tuck it in. "I need to head out. Are you sure you'll be okay? I can tell my family I can't come tonight."

Ben shakes his head. "No, I'll be fine. I'm going to do some homework. My calculus teacher is really riding me hard."

With a wink and a knowing smirk, I cross to him again. "Oh, you have no idea how much harder I could ride you." Using my grip on his hips, I spin him to face the mirror and grind against his ass.

His face and neck flush, and I can't hold back the laugh bubbling in my chest. "God, you're fun to fuck with. So easily riled up." I take a step back, then head out of the room. If I'm going to make it on time, I need to get going. I pull on a jacket, a beanie, and slide my feet into my shoes by the front door. Ben has watched me get ready, I'm not used to it, but it doesn't bother me either. Once I'm ready to go, my wallet, phone, and keys in hand, he approaches me, leaning in for a kiss. This kiss is soft, content, and full of promise.

"Drive safe."

I smile at him. "Always. I'll text you when I'm on my way back. Call or text me if you need help with your homework, or you get bored."

Ben rolls his eyes at me. "I lived by myself for five years. I'll be fine for a few hours." Opening the door, he pushes me out and closes it behind me.

Thirty-Five

BEN

IT'S WEIRD TO BE here when Alister isn't, since I'm basically a guest here. Before getting into my homework, I decided to clean up Kristen and my mess. It's not fair to make Alister clean up when he wasn't involved in making the mess to begin with. Grabbing the trash can and recycling from the kitchen, I set about putting the room to rights.

Empty water bottles have the lids removed and tossed in the recycling, pizza boxes get broken down and thrown in the trash. It's not long before most of the mess is gone, and a few bottles needing to be dumped out are lined up on the counter by the sink. I fold the blankets and put my shoes by the door where Alister keeps his and scan the room. It's such a nice place, so I hate to dirty it up. Content with my cleaning job, I empty the last water bottles and decide to take the trash and recycling down.

Snagging one of Alister's sweaters, my key, and sliding my boots on, I grab the bags and head down to the main floor. The recycling and trash dumpsters are behind the building, but across the alleyway, so getting wet happens when it's raining. Stepping out from under the awning, fat raindrops soak into the sweatshirt while I lift the trash dumpster lid and swing the bag in, doing the same with the recycling.

Turning to head back inside, the back door is closed, and my key won't open it. I sprint out of the alley and into two familiar faces I never wanted to see again, the damn thugs from my old neighborhood. *What the hell are they doing here?*

"Well, well, well. Look who moved on up. How's it going Benny boy?" The condescending tone puts me on edge, the smile full of malice turning my stomach to stone. *I have to get out of here. If they corner me in the alley, I'm as good as dead.* Keeping my mouth shut may help me, but it may make them angrier since I'm not rising to the bait. These two are volatile at best, stupid and violent at worst.

Being a Thursday evening, the street isn't busy, and the rush of people going home is over, leaving me very few options. I know I can't fight them and win, my phone is upstairs, and the only door I can get to is locked.

"North Face? How did you afford that?" short, fat thug asks, a sneer on his face.

"Probably by taking it up the ass," tall, fat thug says, both of them cracking up. "I heard you liked it. You selling yourself now?"

I refuse to respond. It will only be worse if I do. *Just wait for them to get bored and move on.*

"Hey!" tall one yells, startling a jump from me. "I asked you a fucking question, faggot."

Don't respond. Don't respond. Don't respond.

They both take a step closer, shutting down my escape routes. My eyes flick back and forth, looking for anything I can use as a weapon or a way to escape. Since I'm in a nice part of town, the street is mostly clear of debris, leaving me helpless.

Damn thugs keep moving toward me, forcing me back into the darkened alley, lessening my chances of survival with every step. I'm halfway to the dumpsters when the back door opens, and a surprised woman stands there in a bathrobe, holding a bag of trash. Using the distraction to my advantage, I bolt for the door, running as fast as I can. Grabbing the lady's hand, I pull her inside and slam the door shut just as my would-be attackers get close.

Doubled over, breathing hard, I lean against the hallway for a moment before a delicate hand touches my shoulder. "Are you okay?"

My breathing is too labored to speak, so I nod yes and take a few more deep breaths. "Thank you. You may have just saved my life."

She looks panicked for a moment, her hand flying to her heart. "Do I need to call the police?"

"No, they didn't do anything besides threaten me. But I would wait to throw your trash out, because they may be waiting by the door." She nods her head and follows me to the elevator. "I'm Clara, by the way. I live in 2B."

"I'm Ben, and I'm just staying with a friend for a few days in 3F." She smiles at me as if my pathetic life hadn't just flashed before my eyes. The elevator arrives, we select our floors, and the ride is silent. She waves when she gets off on her floor, and I lean back against the railing. The doors open on the third floor and I head back to the apartment, locking and deadbolting the door when I get inside. Finally, able to release the fear, I collapse on the floor in the entryway, hyperventilating.

My heart is pounding painfully against my ribs, my breathing out of control, and my head is screaming. I curl into a ball which has always brought me comfort. With my arms wrapped tight around my knees, my breathing begins to slow. It takes a while to get my mind out of the fight or flight response, but the lingering scent of Alister is helping me calm.

Eventually, I make it up off the floor and into the bedroom where his scent is the strongest. Laying on the bed, I pull his pillow to my chest and curl my body around it. *I'm safe. I'm safe. I am safe...*

Hours later, I'm woken when Alister slides against my back, kissing my neck and rubbing my chest. I'm still curled around his pillow, inhaling his cologne while I slept.

"I'm definitely ready for dessert," Alister whispers in my ear, nipping at the lobe and sucking on it. I gasp in surprise, the electric shot shooting straight to my dick. I want to feel every inch of him against me, skin-to-skin. I need him. It wasn't until right now that I realized exactly how much. Stretching out, my ass pushes against the bulge in his jeans, his appreciative groan reverberating down my spine.

With my arm reaching behind me, I grab a fistful of his hair and arch into him. "Fuck me," I groan out, his hand sliding inside my boxers. "Make me yours."

For only a second, Alister freezes, and then jumps into action, pulling at our clothes. "Off, pants off." My pants and boxers easily slide off, bunching at the foot of the bed with my shirt quickly joining. Rolling toward him, I help Alister lose his clothes, eager hands making quick work of it. Reaching for the bedside table, the top drawer opens and closes quickly. My eyes meet his, and my breath catches in my throat.

Alister climbs back on the bed and claims my lips, demanding entrance to my mouth. He's owning me,

Rescue Me

possessing me, at this moment and I bask in it. To be needed this urgently is something I've never experienced, but I want more of it. With a hand on my hip, he rolls me so my back is to him once again. Chest to my back, his hand slides down my leg and pulls my knee to hook over his, spreading my thighs for him. Lube covered fingers slide against my hole, the anticipation of pleasure making me tense.

"Relax babe. We'll get to the good stuff in just a minute." The growl of Alister's voice has precum forming on my tip. I take a deep breath and relax, and one finger pushes into me, quickly followed by a second. Even the lazy pumps of his fingers have me ready to cum, aching to feel him inside me again.

"Please," I beg, my voice a whimper.

Alister chuckles in my ear and adjusts the angle of our hips to line up his cock. "Do you want my cock?"

"Yes!"

His hardness pushes into me, a steady thrust until he's fully seated, both of us groaning at the tight fit. "Don't stop." My body needs to be worn out, fucked hard. He doesn't question me, just does what I asked. He gives me only a few slow thrusts before he picks up speed, his hips soon slapping against my ass over and over. My back arches, my dick aches, and my balls draw up tight, ready to explode. The orgasm is about to overtake me, my mind spinning out of control, and my body tightening around Alister as he slams into me. The world goes white and silent when the orgasm hits, my arms flying out to find something to hold on to. Jets of cum shoot onto my stomach and the bed, forcing Alister to cum with me. His hips slapping against mine, forcing my body to take what he's giving.

My mind crashes back into my body, and I'm left gasping for air, sweaty, and trembling. Behind me, Alister is panting with his forehead against my shoulder. A smile tugs at my lips, I love that I do this to him, that he wants me this badly. This beautiful, perfect man wants me, the worthless, unlovable orphan.

We lay in the bed for a few long moments, relearning how to breathe, with his arm slung over my waist. He presses soft kisses between my shoulder blades, the hair of his beard tickling my skin and raising goosebumps.

"Let's take a shower. You're a mess."

"It's your fault," I grumble into the blankets.

"I'll accept the blame since it was fucking amazing." He rolls away from me and walks to the bathroom to start the hot water. When he comes back to the bed, and I'm still laying in a pool of my own cum, he swats my ass and makes me jump. "Come on. We have to change the sheets too."

Forcing my body to move, I follow behind him, letting him blindly lead me into the unknown.

Thirty-Six

ALISTER

Thursday night dinner was exactly as I had expected, my mother cooking something delicious, my father and Alex watching some sports event on TV, and Alex ribbing me about Ben. Mom gave me a pass for not bringing him this week since he had been sick, but I was forced to promise he would join us next week. Hopefully, I can convince Ben to join us.

Coming home to find Ben fast asleep, wrapped around my pillow, made my heart pound. He's starting to feel safe here, at least subconsciously, and it couldn't make me happier. When I slid onto the bed behind him, and he asked me to fuck him, to claim him, I was shocked, but all too happy to oblige. The more I'm around him, the more I can see how painful his past was. And the fact that he trusts me with his body is mind-blowing, I will do everything I can to never break his trust. He doesn't give it often. I'm pretty sure Kristen is the only other person he trusts, and I'm happy to earn it. I want to earn it, to work for it.

It's sometime around midnight now, Ben is asleep next to me, but my mind won't quit. Tonight keeps playing in my head. The sex was better than anything I've ever experienced. Not only did it blow the top of my head off, but there was a deeper connection, an emotional one. Ben asked for what he needed.

The thought has me pausing. *Ben asked for what he needed.* That's huge. My heartbeat increases and a smile lifts my lips, *he trusts me*. I've never wanted anyone's trust like I need his. I crave it. I think I'm falling for him, hard. Irrevocably. Head over heels.

A whimper and jerk have me looking at Ben. His face is contorted in pain and fear—he's having a nightmare. Moving to cradle him to my chest, I wrap my arms around him and whisper in his ear, "It's okay. I've got you." Over and over, my hand rubbing big circles on his back as he fights the demons in his head. He's starting to shake and fight against my hold, muttering "no" and "get off."

Grasping his shoulders, I shake him. "Ben, wake up."

He fights me harder, swinging his arms and kicking at the blankets. "Ben! Wake up!" I shake him harder. Suddenly a blood-curdling scream leaves his mouth, and he jerks awake, sweaty and panting. His eyes are crazed, fear racing through his body as he looks for the threat.

"Ben, you're okay. It was just a bad dream." His eyes find mine in the darkened room and tears fall from his lashes. He takes a deep breath, and a sob racks his body when he curls into me. His arms wrap around me and hold so tight it's hard to breathe, and his fingers are digging into my skin. His face is against the crook of my neck, my beard is probably scratching his temple, but he doesn't seem to care. My leg wraps around his hip, and my arms are around his shoulders, holding him just as tightly as he's holding me.

In this moment of vulnerability, pain, and fear, he reached for me. I close my eyes and just hold him, let him work past the nightmare.

"It's not just a dream." His voice is so soft, I'm almost not sure I heard him.

"Memory?"

"Yes." His mouth moves against my skin, hot breath, and sandpaper from his five o'clock shadow scraping my flesh.

"Do you want to talk about it?" Keeping my heart rate calm and the quiver out of my voice is hard if his nightmares are memories, I can only imagine how bad they are. Ben is the strongest man I've ever met, still carrying on after what he's gone through, he's such a sweet person. He doesn't take his hardships out on other people, doesn't belittle others to make himself feel better. He's a better man than most.

"The man I lived with for most of my life was strict. Punishments were harsh to ensure I didn't make the same mistake again." He shuffles around, his arms relax some, but his voice is devoid of emotion.

"He wasn't above corporal punishment. A leather belt was his favorite device, but I was well acquainted with a wooden paddle too. The worst was when I was left to freeze and starve." His voice never raises, and there's no inflection like he's telling a story about someone else. I was never open hand spanked, I can't wrap my brain around a belt or paddle, but freezing? Starving?

"For days, I would sit in my room with no heat, no blanket, and no clothes. It didn't matter what time of year. My fingers and toes would turn purple and blue. If I did something bad enough, he would come in with the belt after my skin was icy. The sting was so much worse…" He trails off, tears running down my chest as he stops. The lump in my throat makes swallowing hard and I don't have words for him.

He's quiet for a few minutes, done talking for now. My fingers run through his shaggy hair and cup the back of his head. Tipping his head back, he finds my eyes, his full of torment and shame.

"It's not your fault, Ben. It's not your fault." More tears hit my skin, and trail down his face as I lean in to kiss him. A soft brushing of lips against lips while we hold each other, both needing the comfort and reassurance of the other. His lips are a little salty from his tears, but it makes this kiss mean more. There's nothing sexual about it, just reaffirming we're here, together.

It's been about a month since Ben's nightmare and midnight confession. We've fallen into an easy routine. In the mornings he has class, and I drive to campus, so we don't leave at the same time or get seen walking together. The other days, we have lunch together before he goes to class. I make coffee and breakfast every morning, and he makes me a peanut butter and jelly sandwich for lunch on the days we don't eat together, then we make dinner together. He's getting pretty good at chopping, but hasn't made it to actual cooking yet. Tomorrow, he's going to Thanksgiving dinner with me at my parents' house. I am both excited for him to meet my parents and terrified of what Alex is going to say.

A knock on my office door is not unexpected. "Come in."

The door opens, a black hoodie peeks through the opening and obsidian eyes meet mine. A smile tugs at my mouth, just the same as it does every time I see him. "Hey, stranger."

He smiles when he comes in and shuts the door behind him, leaning over my desk for a kiss that's not nearly enough. With a sigh and a smirk, he drops down onto the chair, his backpack at his feet.

"Are you ready for the test today?" I ask him, peering around my coffee mug.

He rolls his eyes and scoffs at me. "Depends. Does the test have the same types of questions as the homework and practice test?"

I shrug. "We'll see."

"You're kind of a jerk. Do you know that?" The more time we spend together, the more he teases me. I love every second of it.

"I may have been told that once or twice."

"Well, third times the charm, right?"

Shaking my head at him, I give him what he has come to call, the teacher eye. "Don't you have studying to do?"

Ben stands with a flourish, and his fingertips against his chest reminds me of a debutant. He tells me, with the voice of a woman, "Why, yes I do, professor." Then spins and bends at the hip to get into his backpack. His ass is in my direct line of sight, cupped perfectly by his faded black jeans. When he looks at me over his shoulder and flips his hair out of his face, I'm done for. Leaning forward over my desk, I glide my hand up his inner thigh to cup him.

I'm impressed he stays in character, fake voice and all. "Professor, that's so inappropriate. What will the Dean say?" His words say no, albeit in a fake voice, but his body pushes into my hand. Ben's eyes close and he bites his lower lip. I grip his shaft through the rough fabric and smack his ass with the other, he jumps from the suddenness but moans when I rub the sting away.

A loud laugh in the hallway has me snatching my hands back and running my fingers through my hair. Ben drops to a crouch at the same time, and we both let out a breath. *We need to be more careful. Someone could walk in at any time.*

Thirty-Seven

BEN

BEING ABLE TO PLAY around, joke, and relax with Alister has been amazing. I finally feel like I'm living, not just surviving. I smile and laugh. We cuddle, talk, kiss, then fall asleep wrapped around each other. It's hard to believe people live their entire lives feeling like this, like things are going to be okay. For the first time in my life, I have hope. I want to know what the future will hold.

However, tomorrow is Thanksgiving, and I'm meeting his family. I've seen Alex, but I've never talked to him or looked him in the eye. But parents? The only parents I've met were Kristen's and her father despised me the second he saw me. What if Alister's parents hate me? Will he change his mind about me and kick me out of his apartment? What if I don't fit in with them? He's from an upper middle class family. I don't own clothes without holes in them which have nothing to do with fashion. Since I moved into Alister's, I've been wearing one of his North Face jackets over my sweatshirt to stay warm.

The calculus test sucked, but I'm pretty sure I passed it, at least I hope I did. Since staying with Alister, my grade has improved, along with my understanding of the material, but it's still as fun as pulling teeth. I do not understand how he teaches this shit for fun. Once I'm done, I head back to his office to wait for him, letting myself in with the key he gave me. I'm pretty sure he can get in trouble for making copies of his office key, but what the school doesn't know won't get him in trouble.

At his office, I'm unlocking the door when someone hollers at me. Surprised, I spin around and look for the person who yelled.

"What do you think you're doing?" A well-dressed, grey-haired man with a pinched face asks me, arms crossed over his chest.

"Professor Bennet asked me to grab something from his office." The lie flies out before I've had time to think of a story.

"He just gave you his keys?"

My stomach is in knots, and I'm ready to throw up. "Yes."

"Give me those keys. We'll be going to give Professor Bennet a little visit." He holds his hand out expectantly.

"Can I grab the papers he asked for first?"

The man narrows his eyes and glares at me. I'm not sure what is going to happen, but I need to make this look as real as possible. "Fine, but I'm going in with you."

"Okay." I finish unlocking and opening the door, stepping inside and reaching for the stack of papers on his desk. I have no idea which class these are for, but it's the only thing I've got. "Got it," I say, lifting the stack to show the angry man in the doorway. Locking the door behind me, I hand over my keys and wait for him to check the door. He looks at the keys in his hand for a moment, and I hold my breath. All that's on the key ring is the apartment keys, the office key, and an 'I heart math' key chain Alister found for me.

Pocketing the keys, he turns and storms down the hallway, leaving me to trail after him. The closer we get to the classroom, the more nervous I get. My hands are trembling, the knots in my stomach are so tight it hurts, and I am about ten seconds from chucking my lunch into a trash can.

The door to the classroom is in sight. I'm praying to a deity I've never believed in that it doesn't open. The grumpy man reaches for the door, and it swings open, Alister abruptly stops to avoid hitting him.

"Mr. Rockwell, to what do I owe this pleasure?" I can see he's struggling to keep the surprise and fear off his face when his eyes flick to mine.

"I found this student getting into your office. He claims you gave him your keys." He holds up the keyring to show Alister, who reaches out and takes them. Before he can say anything, I step forward and push the stack of papers at Alister.

"Here's the stack of papers you asked for, Professor." The words are tumbling from my lips faster than normal.

"Thank you, Ben. You've saved me a trip. Have a good night. I'll see you next week." He smiles a tight-lipped, nervous smile, and dismisses me. In a rush to leave, I all but run in the opposite direction.

All the way back to the apartment, I hustle. Frustrated for being scared, angry I have to lie to get through life. I'm almost to the building when something snags my backpack, catching my immediate attention and pulling me off balance. Falling into an alley, I barely catch myself on a dumpster that smells like it's had better days. Turning to look at the entrance of the alley, I see the thugs from my neighborhood blocking my exit. I had a feeling they wouldn't let it go, that they would be back. These damn wanna be thugs cause more damage than actual gangs.

"Hey, faggot," the one in the center says, taking a step forward. *Fuck.* "We're just here to remind you where you come from. Butt fuckers like you, you don't deserve to be happy or live in nice places."

Don't be a smart-ass. Don't be a smart-ass. Don't be a smart-ass.

My mantra continues to run through my head, but I am sick and tired of life using me as a punching bag, giving me something amazing then ripping it from my fingers. I'm sick of hiding in the background and still getting the shit kicked out of me. I'm tired of being scared all the goddamn time. The way I see it, I'm going to get fucked up no matter what I do, so I might as well say what I want.

"You really are as stupid as you look." The words fly out of my mouth before my brain has a chance to catch them.

"What the fuck did you say to me, you fucking faggot? You think you're better than me?" He takes a few more steps toward me, not leaving me room to escape. Fuck it. I may as well earn the ass whooping I'm about to get.

"Yeah, I do think I'm better than you. If this is all you aspire to be, a wannabe thug, getting into trouble, doing time for petty crimes. You're pathetic. You can't even beat up a half starved gay kid by yourself, so you gotta have your buddies for backup."

That does it. He moves faster than I anticipated, and I get a sucker punch to my jaw, then a kidney shot in quick secession. Falling to my knees, he kicks me in the stomach with what feels like steel-toed boots and forces my arm behind my back until my shoulder pops. Pain is screaming through my body, bruises instantly forming on my skin. Screaming while puking with a dislocated shoulder has me choking on vomit. My entire body is throbbing as the assault continues. A hand grabs my hair and slams my head into the metal dumpster, making lights dance behind my eyelids. Another kick to the head and I'm out cold…

A steady beeping is all I can hear and my head is pounding, so opening my eyes is not high on my priority list. There is no part of my body that doesn't hurt in some form: aching, stabbing, and throbbing. It hurts to breathe. I can't roll or shift without shooting pains stealing what little breath I have.

What the hell happened to me? Am I in a hospital? How long have I been here?

Thinking back to what I remember last, I remember the guys in my neighborhood cornering me in an alley behind Alister's apartment building. They figured out I'm gay and I'm living in a better place, so I'm sure they will continue to fuck with me every chance they get. If they find a way inside, I'm sure they'll stake it out, jump me in the hallway.

Slowly, my eyes open to slits. The first thing I see is my worst nightmare, Dan. *How the fuck did he find me?* The beeping on the machine next to me increases as my heart rate picks up.

A nurse comes in before a word is spoken between us. "Oh good, you're awake!" She smiles at me, but my eyes don't leave the wolf in sheep's clothing standing at the end of my bed. At the computer, she goes over all my stats, checking my IV, and recording all my numbers. "How are you feeling?"

"Everything hurts." My words are mumbled, my throat not wanting to work. I want pain meds to take the pain away, but I'm terrified of what *he'll* do if I'm drugged up.

"On a scale of one to ten with ten being the worst pain you can imagine, how would you rate your pain right now?"

I close my eyes, leaning my head back against the plastic wrapped pillow, maybe he's just a hallucination. "Everything hurts," I repeat, my voice weaker than I expected. "My chest… hurts to breath… head is screaming… please, no lights." Thinking past the pain is almost impossible. The lights are turned off and some of the pressure in my head lessons, a welcome relief follows.

"Thank you," I mumble, my eyes still closed. *Maybe Dan was just a nightmare…*

"I'll let the doctor know you're awake, and he should be in to see you in just a few minutes." The nurse's steps are quiet on the tile as she leaves, the soft whoosh of the door closing behind her.

"You're coming with me. Obviously, my lessons weren't ingrained hard enough, so we'll have to start again." Malice drips from every word, bringing down dread heavy on my shoulders. I don't have to open my eyes again to know he's really here.

"How did you find me this time?" It hurts to talk, but I have to know.

The smile that comes over his face has ice flooding my veins. "I have friends in good places, and they keep me informed of your whereabouts. Did you really think I didn't know where you were all this time?"

My body tightens as fear grabs hold of me. "I'm an adult. I don't have to go anywhere with you." The words are a whisper but no less true.

"I am responsible for your upbringing, and I won't have you out in public acting like some queer. You will do as you're told or deal with the consequences."

I know what the consequences will be. Since I'm already hurt, and my body can't take much more, it'll be starvation and hypothermia. I don't have anyone to call to protect me from him, just like when I was ten years old, I'm once again at his mercy.

Thirty-Eight

ALISTER

When I saw Ben with the Dean of Science and Engineering, my heart stopped. I thought for sure we were caught, and I was on my way to getting fired. I have to admit I was impressed with Ben's story. It was quick thinking on his part, though it earned me a stern talking to about giving my office keys to a student.

I hurry home as soon as I'm done getting chastised since I have Ben's keys. It's cold outside, and I don't want him to freeze. I notice some kind of commotion in the alley behind the building but ignore it. Sometimes homeless people camp out back there to try to stay out of the wind. Ben isn't outside when I get to the door, but maybe one of the neighbors let him in since it's cold and windy, someone may have recognized him over the last week. When the elevator opens on my floor, he's not here either. *Where the hell is he?*

Unlocking the front door, I call his name, hoping by some miracle he's here, but I get no response. Looking through the rooms, it's obvious he hasn't been here. *Where would he have gone? Is he so afraid of meeting my parents he ran? He agreed to come, did I push him?*

Pulling my phone from my pocket, I bring up his name and call him, but it goes straight to voicemail. I leave a short message asking him to call me and hang up. I'm starting to really worry, this isn't like him. I don't know where he lived so I can't check there, I don't have a number for Kristen, and I don't want to worry her, the only other place I know of is the pool hall.

I do a Google search for the pool hall we met at and call the number.

"Ball Scratcher's Pool Hall, this is Trisha, how can I help you?"

"Hi Trisha, my name is Alister, I was there a few weeks ago with a guy named Ben Wallace. Do you remember me by chance?" If she doesn't remember me, I doubt she will give me any information.

"Oh, yeah, of course. What can I do for you?"

"Well, I'm trying to find Ben. You haven't seen or heard from him today, have you? I just want to know if he's okay." God, I sound like a crazy ex.

"Oh. No, I haven't. How long has he been missing?" Now she's worried, those protective maternal instincts taking over.

"Just like an hour, I'm probably overreacting. We were supposed to meet up, and he hasn't shown up, his phone went straight to voicemail. I'm sure he's fine."

She lets out a relieved breath. "Oh okay. I'm sure he's fine, probably got caught up doing something."

"Probably, but if you see or hear from him, can you just ask him to give me a call, please?"

"Sure, no problem."

Rescue Me

We say goodbye and hang up. I have a bad feeling something happened to him, but I don't know what to do or where to look for him. Something happened to him, my gut is telling me so. *What if he got lost on his way back? He could have been hit by a car and is lying in a ditch somewhere. Maybe he fell and broke his ankle, his backpack falling into water so his phone got wet. Someone kidnapped him and is going to murder him...*

This is ridiculous. I'm sure he's fine. He knows how to navigate the city, rarely does anyone get hit by a car when they're walking on the sidewalk, and why would anyone want to kidnap him? He's probably just at the library or something, and lost track of time.

Deciding I need to keep busy, I head to the kitchen and start making dinner. I'm sure he'll be here anytime with a reasonable explanation. Pulling out the pot roast, onion, carrots, and potatoes, I get everything ready to go in the oven, pour the onion soup mix, gravy packet, and some beef brother over it all and place it in the oven. In an hour, it will be mouthwatering.

Without much else to do, I pull out the tests from today and get to grading. Before I know it, the buzzer for the oven is going off, and I have a stack of graded tests. *What if something really did happen to him?* I pull the roast out of the oven and try to call him again, but I'm sent straight to voicemail. *It's time to get ahold of Kristen.*

On the laptop, I pull up Facebook and search for Kristen Collins. It doesn't take me long to find the pretty blonde girl I met a few weeks ago. Clicking on her profile, I send her a message.

Hi Kristen, could you give me a call? Here's my number...

Here's hoping she gets the message and calls me back. Leaning back against the couch, I run through everything that happened today. *Did I do something to scare him off? Is he avoiding me?*

My phone rings on the table with an unknown number, and I quickly answer it. "Hello?"

"Hi, Alister?"

"Yes, Kristen?"

"Yup. What's up?" There's a lot of background noise where she is, so it's hard to hear her.

"Have you heard from Ben today?" The desperation in my voice is easy to hear, but I don't care. I need to know he's okay.

"Ben? Not in a few hours. Why?"

"I haven't seen or heard from him in a few hours either. He should have been back from class before me, but he's not. I called his phone, but it goes straight to voicemail. I'm starting to worry."

"That is weird. Look, I'm at the airport on my way up there now. If you hear from him, send me a message, I'll get it when I land, and if I don't get a message from you, I'll let you know when I get there. I'm sure he's okay. He's a survivor." I don't know if she really means it or is just trying to make me feel better, but I believe her.

"Thanks. I really appreciate it."

"Any time, Teach."

We hang up, and I head to the kitchen for food, suddenly it hits me I haven't eaten since lunch, and I'm starving.

Thirty-Nine

BEN BENJAMIN

My head feels like an ice pick has been shoved through my temple. Dan brought me here, to my personal hell. Since I was drugged up, none of the hospital staff would listen when I tried to fight him, not that I was strong enough to put up much resistance. He smiled and charmed the doctor when I told him I didn't want him in the room, and I didn't want to be discharged to him. The doctor bought every lie, every fake smile Dan gave him. I don't even know how long ago it was. Days? Hours?

My entire body aches from the beating I took and from lying on the subfloor of my old room, doesn't help that the pain medication has worn off. I'm sure he confiscated it too, I won't ever see them.

Since I left, he's pulled up the carpet, removed the curtains, and installed more locks on the door—all of which lock from the outside. I'm freezing. Winter in the

Pacific Northwest is mostly highs in the forties and lows in the twenties. There are definitely colder places, but I have zero heat in here, no blankets or even a jacket. My fingers and toes are turning purple, and I'm sure my lips are blue. My teeth chattering hard enough that I'm worried about breaking them.

I'm huddled into a tight ball, trying to keep my body heat in. I'm in the closet, but since he took the doors, it's not helping to keep heat in. At least I got to keep my clothes this time, though he took my shoes and socks. When I lived here, I would have to strip down to my boxers. It didn't matter what time of the year it was or what I had done to piss him off. My clothes were kept in a different room and I would have to ask him for clothes every day, or go to school in what I was given to sleep in. When I was being punished, I would have to strip my bed, fold everything, and stack it in the hallway outside my door before he locked me in. If I made a sound, any noise at all, he would come in with a leather belt and whip every inch of exposed skin he could get to. I've learned how to shut the world out, not speak for days at a time.

Kristen knew I was abused, even called CPS a few times, but they never found anything. My bed would be back together, my clothes being kept in a different room would be explained away, and the marks on my skin would be gone. He knew someone working there, giving him a heads up and making it take weeks for a welfare check, giving him enough time to hide the evidence. The beatings afterward were always worse, Kristen stopped calling once she figured it out.

At some point he'll give me chicken broth, probably room temperature, cold if he's really pissed off, to hold off the starvation that's looming. Unfortunately, starvation and I have been close friends for a long time. Dan knows exactly how long I can go before medical intervention is needed—he knows all the signs.

I don't know how long I've been here, a few hours or an entire day? The pain meds have finally worn off, leaving me in more pain than I can remember ever being in. The cold certainly isn't helping. If I remember correctly, being so fucking cold will make healing take longer since blood flow will slow down as my body tries to protect the vital organs.

What have I ever done to deserve this? At this point, I don't want some great life, to be rich and madly in love with my soulmate. All I want is to be left alone. I want a quiet life, with a job that pays well enough for me to be comfortable. I want to be able to use hot water and a heater, to be able to eat three times a day and to have a warm blanket.

And Alister Bennett. God, do I want him. He is everything I wish I was. I would give anything to be in his apartment, warm, and safe, wrapped in his arms. I crave him. Thinking about the time I spent with him, has tears filling my eyes. I hate my life.

The locks outside the door start turning, alerting me to the incoming shit storm. I can only imagine what Dan has planned for me. The hinges squeak as the door opens, but I don't lift my head to look, I know he's standing there. His steps are heavy on the floorboards as he comes closer, boots on his feet to protect him from the cold and risk of splinters. Suddenly, frigid water is thrown at me. The shriek that leaves me is involuntary and leaves me breathless. The icy water stings my skin, somehow burning my already freezing body.

"Why are you here, Benjamin?" His voice is grating my nerves like sandpaper.

I know I have to come up with an answer that will satisfy him or risk more pain, but what the hell does he want me to say?

Water hits me again, stealing what little breath I have. Apparently, I took too long to answer him. Before thinking through my answer, I blurt out, "I don't know." I immediately know this is not the right answer when I hear the snap of a belt seconds before it slaps my back. Unimaginable pain screams through me, the sting of the leather a minor annoyance compared to the impact on bruised skin and cracked ribs. I'm already limited on how deep of a breath I can take, each one a carefully executed plan, but it's gone the second he strikes me.

"Why are you here, Benjamin?" His voice is calm, as it always is. I've never heard him yell or even raise his voice.

Words scramble around my mind as I try to gain control over something, my breathing, the pain, this entire fucking situation. "Um... to... to learn a lesson."

Forty

ALISTER

Last night was restless, after tossing and turning in bed for a few hours, I got up and paced the apartment. My mind heavy with every possible scenario. I called his phone so many times that I've lost count, and left messages begging him to call me back. At this point, I don't care if he never comes back here, I just want to know he's okay and not lying in a back alley bleeding to death.

Taking my frustration out on the treadmill didn't work, so I took a brutally hot shower, scrubbing my skin raw just to have an outlet for the frustration and helplessness. After getting dressed and leaving a note for Ben on the counter, I head to my parents' house. For it being a major holiday, the traffic is light, and it doesn't take me long to get there. Alex, of course, is already here and stuffing his face with whatever Mom made for snacking this year.

Everyone turns and looks when I walk in, expecting to see Ben with me. "Where's your boyfriend?" Alex says around a mouthful of crackers and cheese.

I have to take a second and swallow before I can answer. "I, um, I don't know." Mom comes to me and hugs me, ushering me to take a seat on the couch next to Dad. Alex walks over and plops down next to me.

"What happened? Anal warts?"

I want to laugh at the joke, but the sound comes out more like a cough. Dropping my shoulders, I look at my fingers in my lap when I reply, "I think he's missing."

My brother's demeanor instantly changes, Officer Bennet immediately taking the place of my smart-ass twin brother. "Why do you think he's missing?" Turning to my mom, he asks her for a pen and paper to take notes.

"He didn't come home after class last night, and his phone goes straight to voicemail."

"Maybe he went to his family's house for the holiday?" It sounds like such a simple answer, but it's not.

"He doesn't have any family. He was a ward of the state."

"Foster parents?"

I shake my head. "I don't know his name, but the man he lived with was abusive. There's no way he would go there for the holiday."

"Friends? Hangouts?" Alex is writing down information on the paper, gathering what he can.

"The only friend I know of is Kristen, and she just flew in late last night. I've talked to her, and she hasn't heard from him either. I called the only hangout I'm aware of, and they hadn't seen him."

"Full name, date of birth if you have it, description and any identifiable marks?"

"Benjamin Wallace, I don't know his middle name or birthday. He's about five foot ten, a hundred and maybe thirty pounds, shaggy black hair, black eyes. And he doesn't have any marks I've noticed, not even freckles."

Alex is still looking at the paper when he pulls out his phone. "Alright, I'll see what I can find out. I can't promise anything, but we might get lucky."

"Thanks."

He wanders off into the back of the house to make a phone call, and my dad hands me a beer. "I'm sure he's alright, but if he's not, Alex will find him."

I nod my head and take a long pull of the dark beer we both love. My stomach is angry, twisting and turning, and my foot is bouncing. I'm sure it's driving my dad nuts, but he doesn't say anything, just keeps bringing me a new beer when the one I have is empty and shoving food at me. The alcohol on a mostly empty and my anxious stomach is not doing me any favors. I'm pretty sure at any moment, I'm going to be reintroduced to the contents of my stomach.

"Okay boys, dinner is ready!" Mom's singsong voice announces from the dining room. I stand up, and the world spins, and I stumble around the room.

"Whoa there," my dad says, wrapping my arm around his shoulders. "Why don't you lay down for a while?"

My stomach is cramping, and saliva is pooling in my mouth as we make our way down the hall. "Bathroom," is the only word I'm able to say before the overwhelming urge to throw up hits. We make it just in time for me to hit my knees and empty my stomach into the ceramic bowl.

Once my stomach is empty and the dry heaving stops, I lean back against the wall and close my eyes. It doesn't take long for me to doze off.

Forty-One

BEN BENJAMIN

My teeth are chattering, my arms and legs are blue, and I can see my breath when I open my eyes. The beating last night was the worst one I can remember, thanks to the previous injuries. I might actually freeze to death this time, I've heard it's a decent way to go, you just fall asleep and don't wake up. At this point, I would love to sleep instead of being knocked unconscious. It's dark outside, but I have no idea what time or what day it is.

Breathing is excruciating, my stomach is both hungry and nauseated, and my head is screaming from the pressure inside my skull. Pictures of Alister in my mind are the only things to keep me company, his smile when he sees me, laughing over my terrible chopping job, the way his lips feel pressed to mine when we say goodnight in bed. The urge to cry is so fucking strong but I know it will physically hurt to do, so I'm forced to hold it in. Not that holding back doesn't hurt either.

I don't know how I lived before him. In the few short weeks we've been together, my entire world has shifted to revolve around him. He makes my life bright, and brings joy and happiness to my dark and pitiful existence. I need him. He makes my heart beat, my lungs inflate. If I ever see him again, I'm going to make sure he knows just how important he is to me. How essential he is to my happiness. How much I love him.

Oh God. Love? Is that what I feel? I don't think I've ever loved anyone before, besides Kristen, and that's an entirely different feeling. He's the first person I want to talk to when something good or bad happens. I feel safe when I'm with him. And right now, while I'm in the worst place I could imagine, he's the only one I want. That has to mean I love him. Right?

The sound of the locks being turned assaults my ears, my heart pounding in my broken and bruised ribcage.

"Benjamin. I see you're finally awake." The voice of the devil has a smile in it. He's enjoying my suffering, my fear. "Since it's Thanksgiving, I've chosen to be nice and brought you hot chicken broth."

My head picks up, he's never brought me broth that was more than room temperature before, and this is not my first holiday being locked in here. "What's the catch?"

"Finally, you're showing some of the smarts I raised you to have. First, tell me why you're here."

"Because bad boys must be punished." My voice is a broken rasp. The saying cuts through me, humiliating and belittling me to the center of who I am. It's been the same since I moved in here when I was ten. I hate it now just as much as I hated it then. I'm sure that's the point.

"Good boy." *When he dies, I'm going to dance on his grave.* "In order to get hot broth, you have to withstand a lit cigar being put out on your skin twenty-three times, one for every year you've been a bad boy. Now, if you pass out, I wait for you to come back around and your broth cools. The longer it takes to get through them all, the colder it will be. The other option is getting a block of frozen broth." He stands and waits for me the mull it over, arms folded in front of him like a schoolboy.

"Fuck you." I know I'm going to instantly regret the words, but maybe it will mean my death will be faster.

He doesn't say anything, but the belt he's wearing is ripped from the loops and snaps against my frozen flesh, instantly raising a welt. I scream from the pain of the belt and from the deep breath against broken ribs. I'm panting and whimpering, trying to slow my breathing back down.

"Would you like to try again?"

"If I withstand all twenty-three burns without passing out, I want you to reheat it. I deserve it hot."

My eyes peek over my knees, watching him think it over. His face gives nothing away, and I hate him even more for always being so damn in control.

"Alright, if you don't pass out, you can have it reheated. Ready?"

I nod and shuffle out of the closet corner, knowing he's going to want full access to my skin. I fucking hate him. I hate everything about him. Why don't bad things happen to the sick fucks of the world?

"On your side, stretch out."

It's not until now that I realize he must have taken my clothes while I was unconscious because now, I'm naked. It's incredibly difficult to force my body to move, to uncurl from the tight ball I've been in. Every muscle in my body protests as I push my legs from my chest.

Above me, Dan pulls a cigar, cutter, and lighter from his pocket. He knew damn well how this was going to go, as he snips off the end and holds it between his lips while he lights it, the stench of tobacco filling the room. He circles me while puffing on the cigar, choosing where the first burn will go, then crouches in front of my stomach. Without any warning, the bright orange tip is pressed against the soft flesh of my abdomen. A scream rips from my throat surprising even me, and the stench of burning skin mixing with tobacco turns my stomach. My knees instinctually try to come up to protect my stomach, but his feet are in the way, I'm sure he planned it that way. My body trembles as my nerves try to assimilate what is happening.

As calm as can be, Dan puts the cigar back between his lips and lights it again, puffing on it to get the bright orange glow before pressing it against me once again. Over and over he does this, never reacting to my screams. None of it fazes him, like he's clipping coupons from the Sunday paper.

Somewhere around the fifteenth mark, he goes to get another cigar, giving me a much-needed break. Panting, in more pain than I can contemplate, I lay on the cold subfloor and think of Alister. *Is he worried about me? Is he looking for me? Is he angry I missed meeting his parents? Does he think I ran to avoid it?*

All too quickly, Dan is back with another fucking cigar and moves to crouch behind me. He's already ruined my chest and stomach, gotten the front of my thighs, so it must be time to ruin the rest of me. Tears have flooded my face, rolling down to drip onto the floor. The burning pushes into me again, agony greets me, but this time, I'm able to curl up. The pressure against the new burns hurts but my mind doesn't care, the fetal position is what it wants.

My back, butt, and thighs get burns by the time he's done. I've made it through them all without passing out, and now I get hot broth, though I doubt my stomach will handle it well. With my luck, I'll throw it all back up and be forced to live with the smell of that as well.

Rescue Me

Without a word, Dan leaves the room, not bothering to lock the door since there's no way in hell I can escape in my condition, and comes back in with a steaming mug. Shifting to my knees, I'm barely able to sit up. My hands are shaking so bad from the pain and cold I almost dump the mug in my lap when he hands it to me. Using both hands on the mug, which is burning my skin, I'm able to bring it to my lips and drink. The liquid scalds my mouth but warms my body from the inside, heat radiating from my stomach. I'm careful to take small sips even though I want to chug it, my empty stomach needs time to adjust.

My body is screaming, every inch of it desperate for relief with none in sight, but I'm able to keep the broth down. No longer does my stomach cramp with hunger pains, and maybe I'll be able to get a little sleep…

Forty-Two

ALISTER

Sunlight shining in my face wakes me, and it takes me looking around for a minute to realize I'm still at my parents' house. My head is pounding, my mouth tastes like shit, and my bladder is screaming for relief. I get up and make my way to the bathroom. I have no idea what time it is or how I ended up in my old bedroom, but I'm betting Alex and Dad had to carry me.

Thinking of Alex reminds me that he was making a call about Ben. I'm done taking a piss and rinsing my mouth, so I head to the living room in search of answers. I need answers. The closer I get to the living room, the more voices I hear, the more confused I get.

"Can you stop thinking with your dick for one second and listen?" a familiar female voice snaps.

"Look, doll face, I can't go barging into someone's house without probable cause, and you saying you *think* Ben's in there is not probable cause," Alex says, his arms crossed over his chest.

"I'm a journalist, so I know what probable cause means. How about you go to the house for a welfare check and see what you can find?" Kristen says, like she's speaking to a child.

"Hang on," I say, both Kristen and Alex turning to look at me. "How or why is Kristen here?"

Alex smirks. "She was blowing up your phone last night, so I answered it. She said she may have information about Ben, so I gave her the address."

I stalk to Kristen, grasping her arms in my hands. "You know where he is?"

"I have a feeling I do. And if I'm right, it's an unbelievably bad thing." She's worried, it's clear on her face.

"Where is he?" My fingers are digging into her arms, I know I need to relax, take a step back, but I can't. I have to know where Ben is.

"If he's missing, really missing, I'm betting his foster father, Dan, has something to do with it."

"Why? Ben doesn't talk about him much, but by the sound of it, he doesn't want to be anywhere near Dan."

She lets out a sigh and quickly wipes away a tear. "I have my own theories on why he does what he does to Ben, but that's all they are, speculation. The things he did to Ben were more than anyone should have to deal with. I tried to help, I really did, but it backfired every time. After we graduated, Ben ran and hid. Dan found him a few times, beat the hell out of him. I wish I understood why Dan was so obsessed, but I could never figure it out."

"What's your theory?" Alex asks.

"Honestly, I think he's gay and hates it. He beats Ben but has never left scars, he would make Ben barter for clothes. It's strange and seems like more than just a power trip."

"Why didn't he go to the police?" Alex is angry, not at Kristen, but at the situation. This is the exact reason he became a police officer to begin with. He wants to help and protect people.

"Because every time he tried, Dan would find out and the beating would be worse. Nothing ever stuck, he was never arrested or even taken in for questioning. Somewhere, there was a dirty cop always willing to help him."

Alex's jaw clenches, and the vein in his temple pulses. "I have to go to the station." He heads to the door but turns at the last minute and points at Kristen. "You do not go anywhere near that house. Do you understand? If I catch you even on the same street, I'll arrest your ass for impeding an investigation. Stay out of it."

Kristen crosses her arms under her chest and cocks a hip, full of defiance. "Trust me, you won't catch me." The gleam in her eye says she's going to do exactly what she was told not to. Alex stalks toward her, head down like a predator.

"Little girl don't test me. You won't like what happens, that's a fucking promise." He's standing so close to her they're almost touching, but she doesn't budge, just lifts her chin at him.

"You don't scare me. Do your job, find my best friend, and we won't have any problems."

With a growl he turns on his heel and stomps out of the house, slamming the door behind him. I chase after him, needing to know if he's found anything.

"Alex! Wait!" He stops in the driveway and turns toward me. "Have you found anything?"

"Do you remember seeing squad cars at your apartment building last night?"

I close my eyes and try to think past the alcohol cloud that has taken over my brain. "Uh, yeah. There was something going on behind the building when I got home. Why? What does that have to do with Ben?"

"I'm pretty sure they were there for Ben. There was a report of an assault taking place in the alley by the dumpsters. The description of the victim matches Ben, but his name is never mentioned. I'm going to talk to the responding officers, something is fishy. I called the hospital he was taken to but they never ID'd him, someone showed up, and he was released. No information." My heart is pounding in my throat, none of this makes any fucking sense.

"Please find him." My voice cracks as I stand here, terrified of what he's going to find.

Alex's hand cups the back of my head and brings my forehead to his. "I'm going to find him, and I promise I won't stop looking until I do."

I nod my head, not able to speak. With a slap on the back, he leaves me standing in the driveway while he goes off to save my man.

I can't stand around and do nothing. I need to *do* something. Anything.

The look of fear and pity on Kristen's face when I enter the house is ripping my heart to shreds. Heading back to my old room, I find some sneakers in the top of the closet and pull them on, before heading outside for a run. I jog down the familiar street, finding my stride as I follow the path I ran as a teenager. It doesn't take long for the anxiety to settle, my mind to clear. I don't have a plan, I don't know how to help Ben, but I trust Alex to do everything he can to save him. The law limits him, but he'll find a way, and he won't stop until Ben is back with me. I have to believe that.

Rescue Me

The sun has set again, and I'm no closer to having Ben back. I left my parents' house and went home, worked out at the gym in my apartment building, took a shower, and cleaned my place from top to bottom. I'm exhausted but can't stop pacing. If I stop moving my mind will fill with every worst-case scenario possible. Ben being beaten and broken, and then left to suffer alone and in pain. A sob steals my breath. He doesn't deserve any of this. I wish I could go back in time to find the baby he was and take him to a good family to raise him. Taking a steadying breath, I get back to pacing.

I'm out of things to do, my apartment has been scrubbed top to bottom, and I'm exhausted. From the front door, down the hall to the spare room, into the bedroom, then through the living room and back to the door. It's going to be a long night…

Forty-Three

BEN BENJAMIN

I WAS ABLE TO get all the broth down before it got cold and didn't throw it up. The burns covering my body feel like they're on fire, but the cold in the room seems to help. The stench of tobacco and burned skin still waft through the room, mixing with stale air, urine, and mildew. If I had the tools, I would start a fire in here, just to feel some warmth before I die. The smoke would knock me out before the flames touched me, hopefully. Even if it didn't, it would be relatively quick.

How long have I been here? Has anyone noticed I'm missing? Does anyone care?

I'm pretty sure I have a concussion. I'm in and out of it, and my head is pounding. It feels like I've been here forever, my time with Alister just a dream. A cruel dream to make me realize just how good my life could be, then shoved back into reality where everything hurts, and everyone wants to make it worse.

Laying on my side to keep pressure off most of the burns, I close my eyes and drift into delirium.

A loud crash jolts me awake, then running and shouts beyond the door make my head pound, because it's so loud, like an elephant stampede. Someone is in the hallway, yelling, "Found it." And others shouting, "Clear," from other rooms.

I understand what's happening. Has Dan invited more sadistic freaks to cause me more pain? Why are they so loud? Don't they know how much it hurts my head? Or is that the point, to cause me more pain? The locks on the door raddle and I curl into the smallest ball my broken body will allow, the burns and bruises screaming in protest.

The door opens, and I scream, flashlights scanning the room, leaving me blinded. People in dark uniforms come in rushing toward me, and I press my back to the wall, trying to get away from them. What do they want? Are they going to hurt me? What's going on?

The one that gets to me first takes off his helmet, and I'm met with the emerald eyes I've longed to see. "Ben? Hey man, I'm so glad to see you. We're going to get you out of here, okay?" I stare at the face, trying to wrap my muddled brain around an Alister look-alike being here in the seventh circle of hell. On his shoulder, the man kneeling in front of me, speaks into a radio. "I've got him, down the hall, second door on the left. I need a medic."

Someone pops up, making me jump, and hands the officer a blanket, a brown blanket. Déjà vu hits me hard. I'm cold, and the clone of Alister in a cop uniform wraps me in a brown blanket. *Who is it? I know that I know who he is... fuck...* the harder I think the more pressure builds behind my eyes. Laying my forehead against my knees, I close my eyes and cover my ears.

"Guys, he looks pretty rough," the officer in front of me says to the guys coming in the door. A blanket is wrapped around me, shutting the cold out and sticking to the open wounds still seeping blood.

"Hey, can you stand, or do we need to lift you onto the stretcher?" a soft feminine voice asks.

I lift my head and peel my eyes open a crack to see the gurney low to the ground. I may be able to get to it. Shifting my weight to my feet, my burns on my back rip off the wall, forcing a scream from my raw throat. In a rush, two guys lift me under the arms and lay me on the stretcher, hurrying me out of the house and into the waiting ambulance.

The lights are bright, and I have to clamp my eyes closed against them, lifting the edge of the blanket to cover my face. The doors slam closed and we start moving. The EMT's are moving around, trying to start an IV, and calling into the hospital. It takes a while, but eventually we get to the ER. They ask me a bunch of questions, but I can barely keep up, answering only a few. Someone takes pity on me and gives me pain meds, letting my body rest while they clean and care for the burns.

A steady beeping makes its way into my drug-induced sleep, waking me. My memory is fuzzy, leaving me unsure of where I am and how I got here. A hand envelops mine: big, strong, and warm. "Ben?"

That voice. That's the voice I've been dreaming of, hearing in my mind. I'm afraid to open my eyes, afraid I'm once again dreaming. Fear courses through me when the memories of Dan hit me, the beeping increasing as my heart pounds.

"Ben, you're okay," Alister's voice says again, and soft lips and the prickle of his beard meet my forehead. I try to move, to keep him close to me, but fire shoots through me as injuries make themselves known. Slowly, I open my eyes, needing to know if he's really here. "Hey, there you are."

He smiles with tears threatening to fall from his lashes. He's perfect, tired, but perfect. I've missed him. I've never craved anything like I crave him. It wasn't until I was once again at Dan's mercy that I realized just how much I need him. I can't live without him.

"Help." My voice is so raw and cracked, I can barely understand myself, but I have to try.

"Help? What do you need?" He hovers over me, ready to do anything I ask.

"You." My hand reaches for his cheek, the soft hairs of his beard tickling my palm. "Love… you." A tear rolls down his cheek as his eyes meet mine, his lips close enough to feel his breath on mine.

"I love you, Ben." A second later, his lips meet mine, not giving me time to respond. A soft caress of lips, careful and sweet.

He ends the kiss and lays his forehead against mine, emerald meeting charcoal. His smile brightens the room, along with my life. Shuffling around onto my side, I move enough for Alister to get onto the bed with me. I need to be wrapped in him, his arms around me, feeling his heartbeat.

I try to talk but cough instead, like swallowing shards of glass. Alister hands me a cup with a straw, and in no time the cup is empty, he refills it for me. Since the first drink, my mouth feels bone dry, and I can't get enough water. Alister fills the cup one more time then tells me to wait a few minutes.

"Lay with me? Please."

"I don't think I'm supposed to. I could hurt you."

"Please."

He looks around the room like someone will jump out and yell at him, then carefully climbs onto the bed and wraps an arm around my waist.

"Don't ever leave me again," he whispers as my eyes close again. "I need you too much." The corners of my mouth lift in a small smile as sleep once again claims me.

I've been in the hospital now for a few days, mostly sleeping as my body tries to heal. The pain meds given to me ensure that I don't dream when I sleep, which I'm grateful for.

Since this is the last week of school, Alister has brought his laptop in so I can try to get some homework done while I'm here. Next week is finals, and I really don't know how I'm going to manage them.

The door to my room opens, and the shining green eyes of Alister meet mine. "Hey, you're awake. How are you feeling?" He leans down to kiss me before sitting on the edge of the bed.

"A little better I think."

"That's great. I talked to your nurse, Nancy, on my way in and she wants you to try to walk a bit today."

"Okay. How about a shower? I feel disgusting."

Nancy walks through the door, striding across the floor like she owns the place. She's got a little bit of an accent, dark smooth skin, and a beautiful smile. "Well good morning there Sleeping Beauty, what do you think about taking a walk today?"

"How about a shower? I'm pretty sure I can smell myself."

"Well now, we can't have that, can we? As long as someone is in the bathroom while you're showering, that should not be a problem, but I'll double check with the doctor, okay?" She raises an eyebrow at me and has a hand on her hip, and I can tell she means business.

"Sounds good. Thank you."

She checks my vitals, my IV bags, and leaves to find out if I can take a shower. The whole time, Alister sits on the bed next to me holding my hand, running his thumb against the back of my hand.

"How did I get here?"

"You don't remember being rescued?" He turns and bends a leg up on the bed, facing me.

"Not really. It was loud, and I would have sworn you were there." Closing my eyes, I try to focus on the details, but it's like I'm missing some of the film to a movie.

Rescue Me

"You saw Alex. He's the one that found you. He told me he tried to talk to you, but you were pretty out of it, the EMT's got you in the ambulance as soon as the house was cleared."

"What happened to Dan?" I hate how my voice shakes when I say his name. He instils fear in me, even from a distance.

"He was arrested, no bail."

Nancy comes in and lets me know I can take a shower as long as I have supervision. "I can sit in there with him," Alister volunteers.

"Perfect, I'll get you all disconnected and ready to go. Take it slow, you haven't been up in a while, and your legs may protest." I didn't think about how long my legs have gone without use, but she's right, my legs will probably just give out on me.

She gets me disconnected from the monitors and IV lines, then her and Alister help me to stand. It's painful, but it also feels good to move. All my muscles are angry at the abuse and lack of use, screaming to let me know just how much so. It's a slow walk, but we make it to the bathroom where Nancy gets a shower stool set up for me along with toiletries. "Thank you, Nancy. I can handle it from here."

She gives Alister a nod and heads out to attend to her other patients. My gown opens and falls to the floor, giving Alister a clear picture of what I've been through. Humiliation weighs heavily on my shoulders, my head dropping to my chest. I will now wear the scars of my torment for the rest of my life. Proof that I'm fucked up, ruined.

A gasp sounds behind me as he sees the full magnitude of my injuries. The air around me moves when Alister comes to stand in front of me. I can't stop myself from turning into the warmth of his hand as he cups my cheek. "This," his voice cracks as he waves his hand up and down my body, "changes nothing. I love you. I need you." He leans down and kisses my forehead, careful not to touch any burns.

My hand's fist in his shirt, my face buried in his chest, and the dam holding my emotions breaks. Hot tears flood his shirt as all the fear, anger, physical, and mental pain slam through me. Through the tears, words tumble from me, a rambling of the horror I lived through.

"Everything hurt so much, I couldn't breathe, my hands and feet went numb with cold, and my head screamed." Alister's arm barely touches my shoulders, afraid of hurting me. "It's always his first move, freezing and starving. My hands and feet turned purple and blue. He comes in asking stupid questions, and when I answer wrong, I get the belt to my frozen skin. The sting on my skin and the slap against my broken ribs was more than I could stand. I don't know how long I was there, how long I prayed for death to take me, to end the suffering." I fall to my knees, Alister dropping to the floor with me, determined not to let me go. Both of his arms are wrapped around my shoulders, holding me together while I fall apart. "Then the burns. The fucking cigars. I hate them. I always hated them. One burn for every year I've been bad. What did I do to deserve this?" My voice breaks and the words stop pouring from me as I scream through the tears. My hands are balled up so tight in his shirt, causing my knuckles to turn white, and my fingers to scream.

"You're okay, Ben. I've got you. I love you." Alister's words keep repeating until I'm weak and the tears stop. Wiping the last of the moisture away, Alister kisses me softly. He gets the shower going and strips out of his clothes, before helping me to sit on the stool in the tub, and then grabbing a cup to rinse me with, so the pressure of the shower head doesn't hit open wounds. He washes me from head to toe, carefully rinsing each burn and washing the skin in between them, blowing on the wounds when they sting from soap and water. Massaging my scalp, neck, and shoulders, trailing his fingers over my skin to make sure all the dirt and grime is gone. Washing me clean of the nightmare.

He takes his time rinsing me off, the hot water feeling amazing on my sensitive skin even when it stings. When the water shuts off, and I'm finally clean, I feel better. My heart and mind lighter, my body tired but resilient.

Forty-Four

ALISTER

BEN HAS BEEN IN the hospital for a week. I have barely been away from him, too anxious to be away from him for long. Since it was the last week of classes, I did have to go in and teach, but it was at least a distraction while I was gone. I took the laptop to the hospital so Ben could let his teachers know that he was in an accident and was unable to make it. They were all pretty nice about it and gave him the finals review they were all doing.

Luckily, he's being released today. It's Sunday morning and Ben has his last finals this week, then we're home free. Waving to the nurses at the nurses station, I continue down the hall to Ben's room, with a bag of clothes for him to wear home and a coffee with cream and sugar, just the way he likes it. Pushing open the door, he's sitting up in his bed, talking to a nurse as she removes his IV and PICC line. He notices the door open and smiles when he sees me.

I drop the bag of clothes on a chair, hand the coffee to him, and kiss him before sitting next to him on the bed. "Good morning, Nancy."

"Good morning, Alister. Happy to be getting your man back today?" The dark-skinned, short nurse is our favorite. Always smiling but takes no crap from anyone.

"You know it." I wink at her, earning myself a chuckle.

"Alright, why don't you go ahead and get dressed? I'll get your discharge paperwork and medications."

"Sounds good. Thank you."

Ben pulls me into him and kisses me hard, a passion-filled slide of lips, and dancing tongues. When we part, both of us are breathing harder, lust coursing through us.

"Let's get you dressed and home, then we can continue this." The timber of my voice is a little lower, noticeable even to me. Ben turns and swings his legs off the bed. Dropping to a crouch, I help him get boxers and loose pants on. The caress of his dick was purely accidental, sort of. The moan he lets out has me hardening, but this is definitely not the place, especially knowing Nancy will be back any minute.

I untie the gown and let it slide down his arms to pool on the floor. The burns are healing, and the bruises have started to fade, but it's no less heartbreaking seeing the proof of what he went through. Someday it'll be easier to see the scars, but today I feel like I should have somehow prevented it from happening. It's bullshit, logically I know that, but it doesn't stop the thoughts. One of my old, soft cotton t-shirts slides over his head and covers all the bandages.

After everything, he ended up with four broken ribs, a bruised sternum, a skull fracture, and major concussion, along with twenty-three second degree burns. Dan was arrested, charged with kidnapping, false imprisonment, and a slew of assault charges. Alex is still looking into who he knew in the bureau that was helping him all those years, and he takes it very personally that there may still be a dirty cop working the streets.

Nancy comes back in with a brown bag full of medication and bandages, explains what needs to be done to care for his burns and how often he needs medication, and sends us home.

The drive is quiet, peaceful, as we get back to our apartment. He tenses up when we pass the alleyway behind our building, not that I blame him. He told me what happened while he was lying in the hospital, afraid to sleep, afraid of nightmares. He's had one every night since we got him back and I'm hoping being back home will be better. Taking the trash out will definitely be my duty from now on, I could never ask him to go back in the alley where he was assaulted.

Riding the elevator up, he leans into me and lays his head on my shoulder. He still tires easily since his mind and body are healing. We enter the apartment, and I usher him to the couch to rest.

"Are you hungry? I can make you something to eat."

"A little bit, just something small, like toast?"

"Sure, how about some eggs to go with?"

He smiles at me as he settles back into the cushions. "That sounds great. Thank you."

Taking the bag of medications into the kitchen, I scramble Ben some eggs and butter some toast for him, and take the plate out to the living room. I come to a stop as I see him passed out. Setting the plate on the table, I cover him with a blanket and sit next to him, pulling him to lay his head in my lap. I turn on the TV, flip through the channels while running my fingers through his hair and fall asleep myself.

Forty-Five

BEN

BEING BACK AT HOME with Alister is an adjustment. It should be easy to remember the feeling of safety and comfort, but it isn't always. I'm glad I had finals to keep my mind occupied the first week back. Getting to campus was tricky since I'm not well enough to walk to and from the apartment, but Alister all but demanded I take an Uber and he paid for them. I hate that I still don't have money, my financial aid finally came through, but my landlord sent me to collections for not paying rent on an apartment I can't live in, so they took all of it.

I'm almost done. Just a few more hours, one more final, and I'll be home free. I filed my paperwork to graduate, ordered my cap and gown, and I'm ready to be done. My eyes close and my head leans back on the chair when Alister comes storming into his office, making me jump.

"Shit, sorry. I didn't mean to startle you." Concern instantly takes over his face.

"It's okay. What's wrong?"

"I was called to a meeting with the board for disciplinary action." He paces the small space with his hands on his hips.

"For what?" He has my full attention now.

"Inappropriate relationship with a student." His eyes bore into mine when he says the words and I sink into the chair, making myself as small as possible. "I told them I quit."

Shock has me standing. "What?"

Alister comes to me, wraps his arm around my waist and lays his hand on the small of my back. "While you were in the hospital, I applied to a few of the other local colleges and universities. I was given a job offer at the University of Washington, Seattle and I accepted. Once final grades are posted for the semester, I'm done here. We won't have to hide our relationship anymore." The smile on his face is contagious, and I find myself smiling too.

"So, you're okay with all this? You're losing your job because of me."

"I always knew this wasn't a job I would have for the long run. It's time to move on and let myself be happy with the man I love."

I lean into him, lifting onto my toes to cover his mouth with mine. This amazing man is willing to give up everything for me, I don't know what I did to deserve him, but I will work hard every day to ensure that I'm worthy.

After my final exam, I wait for Alister in his office, knowing he won't be long behind me. It's Thursday, which means family dinner at the Bennet house, and I'm attending. To say that I'm terrified is an understatement. Mrs. Bennet called and talked to me while I was in the hospital, I don't remember much of the conversation since I was still on heavy drugs, but I sincerely hope I didn't talk about fucking her son. Alex also came in and took my official statement, but he was all business, so I don't know what to expect from him.

I'm still very easily tired, and simple tasks wear me out, so I'm half asleep when Alister enters his office and kisses my forehead. My lips lift in a smile at the tickle of his beard against my skin.

"Come on sleepy head, we have dinner to get to." He laces his fingers through mine and pulls me to standing. Alister turns to the filing cabinet and collects all the finals he has to correct, and puts them in his bag before we leave the room, and locks the door. For the first time, we walk across campus hand in hand to the parking lot. There aren't a lot of people around, but we still get some looks, groups whispering as we walk past, but we don't pay them any attention.

The drive is quiet after stopping to pick up beer and flowers, our fingers still intertwined and resting on his thigh. The closer we get, the more nervous I get. *What if they hate me? What if they take one look at me and think how much better Alister can do? Will they think I'm just a gold-digging freeloader who's just trying to get a passing grade?*

In the driveway of his childhood home, we sit in silence in his car. "My mother is going to love you," he tells me, turning to face me.

"My own mother didn't love me, so why would yours?" My question is a whisper as I take in the perfect family home on a nice, quiet street.

"You don't know what caused your mother to give you up, but I know my mother and I can promise you, she will love you."

My only response is a nod. He squeezes my hand, and I turn to look at our hands. Alister is the only person who has wanted to hold my hand. I can feel his gaze on my face, reading the thoughts that plague my mind.

I finally lift my face to his, tears welling up in my eyes. With his free hand, he cups my cheek. I nuzzle into his palm, kissing the flesh under his thumb. Arousal hums through my body and blood surges to my dick. Bringing my face toward him, he takes my lips in a hard kiss.

My lips slide over his, my body angling toward his. I untangle our fingers to lean over him, throwing my leg over his to straddle his lap. His cock is just as hard as mine, rubbing against his lower abdomen, forcing a growl from his chest. One of his hands fists in my shaggy hair, and the other grabs my ass, encouraging me to grind against him.

Alister's grunts and moans are going to be my undoing, I'm going to cum in my jeans like a fucking teenager. Ripping his lips from mine he says, "You're killing me." His breathing is heavy and his voice is rough with arousal. The desire to let him fuck me in the back seat of the car is almost overwhelming.

"I want to cum," I whine, helpless to the sensations rioting through me for the first time in weeks. "I need to cum."

Gripping my hips with a bruising squeeze, he forces me to stop. "In the backseat," he orders.

Climbing between the seats is much easier for me than it is for him. "Lean against the door, one foot on the floor." Settling between my legs, his upper half is on the seat while his legs are on the floor.

He lifts my shirt, licking, nipping, and kissing my stomach, as he inches his way to the waistband of my jeans. My hips jerk and lift at random when the anticipation gets to be too much. Unbuttoning and unzipping my jeans, he finally frees my erection. He grips the base of me and strokes root to tip a few times.

"Please," I groan gripping his hair.

Teasing me, he draws out the pleasure. The risk of being caught makes this so much hotter. Since we're pressed for time, he doesn't tease me too long and wraps his lips around my swollen head and swallows. My hips jerk off the seat, forcing my cock farther down his throat. He groans around it, sending electric sparks up my spine. He lifts off and slams his mouth on me again, his mouth open wide to relax his throat, and his tongue on my balls at the same time saliva drips down my length. My cock gets harder, and my breathing catches in my throat, as I struggle to warn him about the impending orgasm.

"Cum… fuck… cumming!" Hot jets of cum fill his mouth as I jerk off the seat with the force of my orgasm. With a hand on my balls, he gently squeezes and sucks down the last of it. Sitting up on his knees, a knowing smile covers his face. I'm leaning against the door breathing hard, completely spent.

"Come on, put your dick away, it's time for dinner." He wipes his mouth to make sure there's no evidence left before opening the door and climbing out. I straighten my clothes, get tucked away, and exit the car behind him.

I can feel the flush heating my cheeks when I look up at him. "Thanks." It's the best thing I can come up with. My synapses are still misfiring after the explosion that just occurred. My hand is wrapped in his as he leads me to the front door of his parents' house, the home he grew up in. I wish I knew what it was like to have lived in the same house my entire life, have happy memories associated with it.

Before we get to the porch, the door opens, and Alex is standing in the doorway with a knowing smile on his face. *Since Alex and Alister have the same face, does this mean their smiles and smirks mean the same things too?*

"Having a little *pep talk* in the driveway?" He smirks at Alister. *Oh shit. He knows.*

"Keep it up, and I'll recreate it for you to watch," Alister responds, walking past his twin brother without a backward glance. The look on Alex's face reminds me of someone who smelled rancid milk, followed by a full body shudder. Between the embarrassment of being caught and the reaction from Alex at Alister's threat, I start to laugh. Once the laugh starts, I can't seem to stop it. Soon I'm doubled over in the entryway, holding my stomach, trying to get it under control before the pain in my ribs gets too bad, and failing. Tears are pouring down my face, my lungs burning from trying not to take too deep of a breath, and my knees drop me to the floor.

Alex and Alister both drop down into a crouch, the same confused, amused look on their faces, and I lose it again. "Oh, God, it hurts." I'm finally able to get out between bursts of laughter. The pain in my ribs making it easier to get it under control.

My hands wipe the tears away, and I look up at the brothers, both of them raising an eyebrow at the same time. "Okay, it's weird when you do that."

"Do what?" they repeat in unison. They look at each other and chuckle.

"Come on, let's get you off the floor, ya lunatic." Alister reaches out a hand for me to help me up, which I'm grateful for.

Rescue Me

Alister wraps an arm around my waist, leading me deeper into the house and to the living room where his father is sitting on the couch watching football.

"Dad, this is Ben. Ben, my father, David." He introduces us, and the older version of Alex and Alister stands to shake my hand.

"It's nice to meet you." He has an easygoing way to him, and a warm smile that helps me relax. I'm not sure what I was expecting from him, but this wasn't it.

"He's Ali's boyfriend," Alex pipes up from behind me, causing me to jump.

David sighs and looks at Alex with boredom. "Really? I assumed he was Alister's landlord." Everyone chuckles when he shakes his head and sits back down, muttering something about where they went wrong with him.

Moving into the kitchen, Alister leans in to kiss his mother's cheek. "Hi, Mom, this is Ben. Ben, my mother, Jane." The short, willowy woman with light blonde hair and a skirt that twirls around her ankles is completely at home here in the kitchen.

"I'm so glad to finally meet you!" she says, wrapping her arms around me in a tight hug. I try not to tense up, but she squeezes my ribs, making me wince.

"Oh no, I'm so sorry!" she says, letting go of me instantly. "Do you need anything?"

"I'm okay, did you say finally? Finally, meet me?" Alister and I have only been seeing each other for a few weeks, two months tops.

Her laugh is soft and twinkles. "Yes, dear, that's what I said. I've been trying to get Alister to bring you to dinner since the first week of the quarter."

Turning to him, I see his cheeks are tinged pink. For the first time, he's embarrassed. "You told your family about me?"

Alister wraps his arm around my waist again, carefully pulling me into him. "That first time, they bombarded me until I told them about the student that caught my attention on the first day of school. After that, I was forced to give weekly updates." He shrugs like it's not a big deal. "My family doesn't care that I'm gay, though Alex does love to give me a hard time and has an endless supply of gay jokes."

Before I can respond, Jane is kicking her sons out of the kitchen. "It's time for me to talk to him, you've had him all to yourself for weeks," she informs Alister, who lets out a sigh and walks away.

"How are you doing? The boys have told me some of what you've recently gone through." Her gaze softens, becoming maternal.

"Oh, they did?"

"I'm a child psychologist, I've worked with kids in the foster care system for almost forty years now, there isn't much I haven't heard at this point. They still come to me when they need help, when they need to process. Your recent trauma was very hard on both of them, for different reasons, of course." She goes back to stirring the pot on the stove. A whiff of chicken broth hits me, my stomach instantly revolting, violently.

Spinning on my heel, my hand over my mouth, I look around for a bathroom and hurry toward a hallway. Behind me, I can hear Alister and Jane calling my name. Alister makes it to me first, pushing a door open and flipping on the light as I hit my knees in front of a toilet. My head is spinning with memories of Dan—frigid temperatures, the stench of cigars and burning flesh, and searing pain.

My stomach empties into the bowl, my ribs screaming as they are forced to contract. "Ben? Are you okay?" Alister kneels behind me, gently rubbing my back and puts a cool, wet washrag on my forehead.

My entire body is shaking as I fight through the memories to get back to the present. "I'm sorry." The words automatically tumble from my lips. I've caused a problem, offended his mom, and I don't know how to make it right. The first response is always to apologize. I've been conditioned to do it.

"Sorry for what? Being sick?"

Leaning back into the warmth of Alister's chest, I turn my head into his neck and inhale a deep breath. Cinnamon and nutmeg help clear the fog from my mind.

"I can't eat dinner."

"Are you sick? I can take you home." His hand comes up to feel my face, checking for a fever.

"No, it's soup." I know I'm not making any sense, but I can't get the words out right. A knock on the door startles me, causing Alister's arm to pull me closer to him.

"It's okay, you're alright." He opens the door, and I can see Jane's skirt over his shoulder.

"How's he doing?" Her voice is full of concern.

"I'm not really sure, can I get some water and bread or crackers?" he asks.

The door closes, and I close my eyes. "I can't eat chicken soup."

The door reopens, and I'm handed a dinner roll and a bottle of water. "Thank you."

"You're very welcome, dear." The door closes again, and she's gone.

"So, no chicken soup."

"Whenever I was being punished, the only thing Dan would give me to ward off starvation and dehydration was chicken broth." *Why can't I just be normal, be like everyone else?*

"Jesus," he mutters under his breath, hugging me tightly to his chest. "Okay, no chicken broth. We can do that."

A tear trickles down my cheek and onto his shirt. "I'm sorry," I whisper and take a drink of the water.

Alister's fingers lift my chin, my eyes meeting his. "You have nothing to be sorry about. You're a survivor, and we'll get through this, I promise."

"I love you."

He smiles a soft smile. "I love you, too. Now let's get out of here."

I nod my head, and we stand, leaving the safety of the bathroom and head to the kitchen where Jane is putting the cover back on the soup pot. "How are you feeling, dear?"

"Better, sorry about that."

"No need to apologize, you did nothing wrong," she says matter-of-factly.

"Mom, Ben can't eat chicken broth, can I make him a sandwich or something?" Alister quickly steps in to help me.

"Oh, I'm so sorry, I didn't know that. I will remember that for next time. I can make a sandwich, or I have leftovers if you would rather have that." She starts pulling containers out of the fridge and stacking them on the counter, pulls down a plate, and fills it with more food than I can possibly eat. "Have a seat in the living room, and I'll let you know when dinner is ready."

Heading to the couch with Alister, I feel a sense of relief telling me everything is going to be okay. That I've found somewhere, I can belong, where I'm accepted, and cared about. I don't need to give an explanation for why I can't or won't eat chicken broth, it's just accepted. Just like that, I feel like I can have a family.

Epilogue

ALISTER

June - Graduation Day

Half asleep, I feel Ben move against my back, his dick hard and cradled between my ass cheeks. We've been sleeping naked since we discovered being skin to skin helps with his nightmares. All his physical injuries have healed, but the psychological damage we take one day at a time. He's getting better, has more good days than bad ones, and talking to a therapist has been wonderful for him. My mom recommended someone, and the two of them clicked at their first meeting.

Ben moans behind me, his hips pressing harder against me. He's never taken me, but I'm happy to let him. Reaching back, my hand finds his head and tangles in his hair, using the leverage to pull him closer. "Take what you want. I trust you." My voice a growl. A whimper leaves his lips, his hands gripping the skin at my hips. My hand doesn't leave his hair when I roll onto my stomach then up to my hands and knees. He gets to his knees and sits up, still gripping my hips and thrusting against my ass. Reaching for the side table, I grab the lube from the drawer and hand it back. When he hesitates, I look back at him. He's fighting with himself, I can see it clear as day, as lust, fear, and uncertainty all fight behind his eyes.

"Ben." His eyes snap to mine at his name. "Do you want to fuck me? Right now, at this moment, is that what you want?"

"Yes." His answer is quick, no thought needed.

"Then do it."

He takes the bottle, flicks the cap open and dribbles some in between my cheeks, the cold liquid making me shiver. Spreading my legs to give him better access, he drags his tip through the moisture and lines himself up. The anticipation is killing me, making me tense, but when he pushes against the tight ring of muscle, I lean back into him. "Oh fuck," tumbles from my lips, the burn and stretch both pain and pleasure. My butt stops when it hits his hips, and my head drops to hang from my shoulders. I have to force myself to be still, to not take control—he needs this.

Ben's hands caress my back, giving me time to adjust to the cock in my ass. "Please move. Please, fucking move."

He takes pity on me and pulls almost all the way out, the slide made easier by the lube, the friction leaving stars bursting behind my eyes. When he pushes back in, it's harder this time, faster, going deeper. His groans feed my lust, I want him to feel good, and I want to be the reason. Within a few thrusts, he finds a rhythm that hits everything right. My orgasm is building, my balls heavy and drawn up, my cock hard as steel and hasn't been touched, but that won't stop the explosion.

Ben jerks and loses the smooth slide, his orgasm erupting inside of me, almost leaving me hanging. Grabbing my cock, I fist it tight, stroking only twice before shooting cum onto the sheet under me. Breathless and sated, Ben collapses next to me on the bed. A lazy smile lifts my lips even with my breathing and heart rate through the roof. It takes me a minute, but I make my way over to Ben and kiss him, a soft, lazy kiss.

"Let's get in the shower," I say against his chest, biting his nipple. His back arches and a hiss leaves his lips.

Slowly, I force my body to move and walk into the bathroom to turn the water on. I take care of business and am leaning against the sink when his eyes appear over my shoulder, looking devious.

"What are you up to?" My eyes meet his in the mirror.

"I just fucked you."

I chuckle and smirk. "You did a damn fine job of it too."

His teeth sink into the meat of my shoulder, forcing a hiss from me this time, before he steps under the spray. I step in behind him, watching the water cascade down his body. The burn scars don't detract from the perfect lines of his body. He's started working out with me and is eating right, so he's filling out with lean muscle like a swimmer's body, long and lean, but strong.

My hand reaches out, tracing the lines of muscle on his chest and abdomen, cupping his length and stroking it to hard again. I can't get enough of him. I came not five minutes ago, but I want him again, this time with me in charge.

"Oh fuck." Ben's whine turns my semi into raging steel. I need him now. Grabbing a fistful of hair at the back of his neck, my mouth ravages his, demanding entrance with love bites and nips. Letting go of his cock, my hand slides around to cup his ass, grinding our hips together.

His arms slide up my chest, playing with my nipples before hooking around my neck. Against his lips, I say, "Up," while my hands cup the back of his thighs. Jumping up, his legs wrap around my waist, and I lean his heated back against the cool tile. Grabbing shampoo, I lube up his hole and push my way inside, giving him no prep work. Ben's lips rip from mine, a moan crawling from his throat as I fuck his ass. My hands cup his ass cheeks, using them as leverage to fuck him the way I want to—hard and out of control. I want him mindless with lust, not able to think about anything but my cock buried deep inside of him.

"Please Alister, harder." His head is thrown back against the wall, eyes squeezed tight, as he begs me. I'm all too happy to oblige.

My pace picks up, thrusting into the hot, slick ass that grips me perfectly. "You were made to take my cock."

"Yes." His whine almost pushes me over the edge.

"Marry me." The words fly from my mouth mid-thrust.

"Wha… what?" It takes him a second, but his eyes meet mine, my rhythm never faltering.

"Marry me, make me the happiest man in the world." My words are grunts, barely recognizable.

"Yes!" he shouts as the angle changes, hitting him just right. "Yes. Yes, I'll marry you. Now fuck me like you mean it."

Harder and harder, I'm slamming into him, taking him like the savage he brings out in me. At this pace, it doesn't take long for him to cum, spraying both of us with the sticky, hot liquid. The tightening of his ass around my cock pushes me over the edge and I fill his ass with my seed. I collapse to my knees, my dick still buried in him as we sit on the floor of the shower. The hot water is pouring over us, relaxing us even further.

"Were you serious? About wanting to marry me?"

"Of course I was serious." Sitting up, he searches my face. "I love you, Ben. I can't live without you. I want, no, *need* you to be mine in every way possible."

A smile covers his face, shines in his dark eyes. He cups the back of my head and kisses me soft and slow, then lays his forehead against mine. "Ditto."

I chuckle then kiss him quickly. "We better finish up before the water turns cold."

"Don't worry. I'll keep you warm."

Ben

"Congratulations class of 2019. You did it."

The stands erupt with cheering, and we all stand from our chairs in caps and gowns. With my diploma in hand, I make my way through the throng of people to the meet up location I set up with Alister. It takes a while to get there, but eventually I see the smiling face of my fiancé surrounded by his family and my best friend. Running for him, I wrap my arms around his neck, hugging him tightly.

"Congratulations, babe. I'm so proud of you," he says before kissing me.

"Thank you." The smile on my own face is bright and full of happiness.

Taking a step back, Kristen tackles me, shrieking, "we graduated! I can't believe we're finally done!"

"Now we have to get jobs and be adults!"

The Bennet family congratulates me with slaps on the back and hugs, Jane with happy tears in her eyes. When everyone is done, Alister pulls me to his side with an arm around me.

"We have an announcement to make," he starts, smiling down at me. Everyone stops talking and looks between us. "We're getting married."

Another round of congratulations and hugs ensue, and my heart is full and happy.

Kristen grips my head in her hands, forcing me to look a her. "Do you believe me now?"

"Believe what?"

"That you're fucking worth it."

I smile at her, my throat clogged with tears as I nod. I pull her into a tight hug and she squeezes me back just as hard.

I've finally found a family, been accepted as one of them, and I'm loved. This amazing group of people took me in, damaged and broken, loved me at my worst and helped shape me into the man I am today. I will always be indebted to them, they've done more for me than they realize, and it's a debt I won't ever be able to repay, but I won't ever stop trying. This family chose me, and it's so much better than what a lot of people are born into.

Kristen and Alex have an adventure of their own in Curves Ahead, one click it today!

Books2read.com/CurvesAhead

Other Books

Craze
Learning Curve
Curves Ahead

By Andi Jaxon and AJ Alexander
Save Me

The SEAL'ed Series
Honor
Love
Fate
Power
Faith
SEAL'ed Boxed Set

About

From Dyslexic kid with a love of Algebra to a published author, no one is more surprised than I am. I love to write about tortured pasts and hot sex, a happily ever after that has to be worked for. My stories tend to be a little dark but with some comic relief, typically in the form of sarcasm.

Want to know more about Andi Jaxon? Follow me on social media or subscribe to my mailing list to receive the latest information on new releases, sales, and more!

Amazon: https://www.amazon.com/author/andijaxon
BookBub: https://www.bookbub.com/profile/andi-jaxon
Goodreads: http://www.goodreads.com/andijaxon
Facebook: http://www.facebook.com/andijaxonauthor
Instagram: http://www.instagram.com/andijaxon
Website: http://www.andijaxon.com
Newsletter: http://bit.ly/AndiJNewsletter

Printed in Great Britain
by Amazon